NOW

YOU'RE

MINE

T0384224

NOW YOU'RE MINE

MORGAN BRIDGES

FOREVER

New York   Boston

Forever
Hachette Book Group
1290 Avenue of the Americas, New York, NY 10104
read-forever.com
@readforeverpub

Originally published in trade paperback and ebook in 2023
First Forever trade paperback edition: October 2024

Forever is an imprint of Grand Central Publishing. The Forever name and logo are registered trademarks of Hachette Book Group, Inc.

The publisher is not responsible for websites (or their content) that are not owned by the publisher.

The Hachette Speakers Bureau provides a wide range of authors for speaking events. To find out more, go to hachettespeakersbureau.com or email HachetteSpeakers@hbgusa.com.

Forever books may be purchased in bulk for business, educational, or promotional use. For information, please contact your local bookseller or the Hachette Book Group Special Markets Department at special.markets@hbgusa.com.

Character illustration by Skadior Art

Library of Congress Control Number: 2024938160

ISBNs: 9781538772140 (trade paperback), 9781538772133 (ebook)

Printed in the United States of America

CCR

10 9 8 7 6 5 4

To the readers who want all the smut...
You're welcome.

CONTENT GUIDANCE

The contents of this dark romance book may be triggering to some readers. It contains explicit sexual content and a morally gray hero who's over-the-top jealous/possessive, a stalker who falls first *and* harder and is willing to do whatever it takes to have the heroine.

Trigger warnings include the following:
Violence, murder, grief, stalking, death of a parent, mentions of involuntary drug use, mentions of assault (physical and sexual)

Welcome to the Dark Side.

CHAPTER 1

C alista

I CAN'T DO THIS.

The emotional pain of Hayden's betrayal courses through me. Tremors wrack my body, and the pearls in my hand clink against one another. The tiny sound is like the banging of a drum. Or is that my heart? I could've sworn it stopped beating the minute he entered the penthouse.

And looked desperate to touch me.

I take a fortifying breath and lift my chin. If I don't confront him now, I never will.

"Where did you get these, Hayden?" I repeat the question I asked a moment ago, my voice still shaking but my resolve firmly in place. "I need to know."

He holds my gaze, the detachment in his eyes gutting me. "You already do."

I shake my head, either in denial or as a response; I'm

not sure which. "No, what I have is a suspicion that needs confirmation."

"What do you want me to say, Calista?"

His use of my full name has me wincing. I quickly school my features and fist the pearls to place my hand on my hip. "The truth. That's all I want from you."

"You don't know what you want." He averts his gaze in a rare show of uncertainty. "And it doesn't matter until I find out who's behind your assault."

From one blink to the next, my agony morphs into anger. "*What?*"

Hayden brings his attention to me. This time it's with the full weight of his stare. It settles on me, pressing in from all sides until I'm hunching my shoulders. The unspoken thoughts running through his mind make the silence deafening, and I almost wish I hadn't confronted him.

"Never mind," he says, squeezing the bridge of his nose. "Keeping you safe is the only thing that's important."

"How can I be safe with you when *you're* the one who's been stalking me?"

"I did it to protect you. Whether or not you choose to accept that is your prerogative."

I huff. "Explain how scaring the shit out of me was for my protection."

"Language, Cal—"

"Fuck language, and fuck these roundabout answers," I say, my words one decibel away from a shout. "Tell me how someone can justify breaking into my apartment, stealing my shit, and then have the fucking nerve to say it was for my own good."

Hayden's gaze flashes right before he grabs me by the shoulders and yanks me to him. "Don't you realize how vulnerable you were walking in the city at night? Do you know what could've happened if I hadn't been there to watch over you? Or is that a truth you don't want to acknowledge?"

I shove at his chest. It's as effective as pushing a mountain, and I drop my arms in defeat, still clutching the pearls. "I didn't have a choice. I'm sure it's easy to pass judgment from your penthouse. You can say whatever you want, but I don't believe my safety is the only issue here."

He lowers his head until our faces are mere inches from one another, our breaths mingling. "I wanted to fuck you," he says, his tone guttural and deep. "I wanted you more than I'd ever wanted a woman in my life. I broke into your apartment and took your necklace to stop myself from taking your body. So yes, I wanted to keep you safe from the world, but also from myself and what I would do to you."

"And now that you've fucked me? Is your obsession gone?"

He releases a sardonic laugh that has my skin prickling. "Gone? Oh no, my sweet little bird, my obsession with you has only gotten worse."

His words kick-start my heart like I've taken a shot of adrenaline. The idea of Hayden watching over me like a deranged bodyguard gives way to an incessant throbbing at my temples, one that has me gritting my teeth and sucking in a breath. With my entire body rigid, except for the rise and fall of my chest, I stand there, unable to do anything except feel overwhelmed by Hayden's desire for me.

And my fear of him.

I don't think he'd hurt me physically. The things that scare me are the depth and intensity of his commitment. Do I have it in me to embrace this side of him? Do I even want to?

"Were you ever going to tell me?" I whisper.

"No."

The truth of his response is like a smack to the face, and I rear back in his hold. "How can I trust you when I know you'll lie to me?"

"I will lie, cheat, steal, and kill if that's what it takes to keep you. You're all that matters to me."

"Even if I hate you for it?"

He flinches at the question, as if taking a bullet to the chest. "You can hate me for now, but not forever."

"You can't control that, Hayden."

"True," he says between clenched teeth. "But I can control everything else."

I drop my gaze, not wanting him to see the agony that's sure to be in my eyes. This man admitted that he wanted to possess me, and I ran. Do I have the strength to try again? Does it matter when my chances of success are minimal and part of me doesn't want to leave in the first place?

I've never understood how a person could love and hate someone simultaneously, but Hayden has enlightened me.

"Let go of me," I say, my voice calm despite my inner turmoil.

Hayden places his index finger under my chin to lift my head. "Never."

I stare up at him, not bothering to conceal my fury. "I don't want you touching me right now."

"Miss Green, I wish you would try to stop me."

The futility of my situation rises like steam to heat me all over. I shrug from his hold, but his grip is too strong, frustrating me all the more. In one last-ditch effort to get free, I fling the pearls at him. The iridescent orbs hit him in the face and his chest, bouncing off to clink on the floor.

He releases me. I press my lips together to keep my jaw from dropping, unable to believe that worked. Without his hands on me, my thoughts clear, and I can put this fucked-up situation into perspective.

"Hayden, I care about you. More than I want to admit right now." When he quirks a brow in disapproval, my stomach dips. "But you have to see this from my point of view. How would you like it if someone violated your trust and invaded your privacy?"

"Everything is about motivation. If a mother kills someone for hurting her child, would you condemn her?"

I shake my head. "That's different. She didn't hurt the person she loved."

He stiffens.

"Regardless if you want to admit it or not, you've hurt me with your actions. I need time to..."

"To. What?" he asks, the words clipped.

"To figure out if I can move past this."

Hayden smirks and the mocking expression has the hairs on my arms lifting. "And if you can't?"

"I—I don't know."

"Let me be clear, Miss Green. That's *not* an option." He leans forward, placing his lips by my ear. "You can run, but I'll *always* chase you."

I take a step back, and he lifts his head, his gaze trailing my every movement as I cross my arms. The action is nothing more than a thinly veiled attempt to put a barrier between us, but I need distance from him in any way I can.

"You can come after me physically, but here?" I say, pointing to my temple. "This is a place you can't follow me, no matter what you do."

He frowns, his confident air disappearing. The blues of his eyes glitter with uncertainty and something I've never seen—fear. It stabs me, cracking the facade of bravery I'm shielding myself with.

"Hayden," I say, struggling to keep my voice stern, "there's nothing left to talk about. We're at an impasse."

He doesn't move, not even to acknowledge what I've said. Or maybe that's on purpose to show he disagrees.

"I'm going to call it a night," I say.

"But you haven't eaten."

I shrug. "I can't when I'm upset."

"Upset" might be the understatement of the year. My brain is so muddled, I don't know if I can chew and swallow food without choking. From the way my thoughts are buzzing in my skull, I doubt that I'll sleep tonight.

"You're going to eat, even if I have to force-feed you," he says, his tone leaving no room for argument. "Now, you can either walk into the kitchen, or I can carry you there, but either way, you're going."

Righteous indignation causes me to lift my chin with a dainty sniff. "Fine."

I don't wait for him. My bare feet sink into the plush carpet with every step until I reach the cold tile in the kitchen. The stark change in temperature against my soles sends a chill through me, but not more than the predatory man trailing me. Although I can't hear him walking, I can sense him.

I always do.

"Do you have a preference tonight?" he asks.

Turning to look at him, I shake my head. "It doesn't matter what you give me. I won't enjoy it."

"Miss Green, you'll enjoy *anything* I stick in that pretty mouth." When I press my lips together, he smirks at me. "Have a seat."

My pride, already raw from his lies, chafes at the command. I cross my arms and give him a pointed stare. His gaze narrows to little more than slits.

"Sit. Down."

I continue holding his stare, begging my inner fortitude to remain strong. Backing down is not an option. Not when this man has taken possession of me in more ways than I care to admit.

He's on me from one blink to the next, moving too fast for my brain to process. I let out a shriek at the feel of his hands grabbing my waist. He lifts me onto the island, his fingertips digging into the fabric of my jeans. I chose to wear them and a plain blouse instead of Hayden's clothes. Once I found the pearls in his pocket, I couldn't get the coat off fast enough.

I glare up at him, unable to keep my breathing even while agitation rushes through me. My chest heaves with every inhale, and he drops his gaze to the hint of cleavage my top displays. I resist the urge to pull the neckline up.

"My eyes are up here."

His lips twitch. "I'm not going to apologize."

"Then what are you doing?"

"Making sure you stay put."

I huff. "I'm not going anywhere."

"It's good to hear you accept the inevitable," he says, "because now you're mine."

CHAPTER 2

C alista

HAYDEN'S WORDS WRAP AROUND ME LIKE A RIBBON, SILKY YET binding.

He watches me for a moment, as if challenging me to jump off the island. I've already fucked around and found out. I'm not interested in another lesson.

Before I can think of a response, he walks over to the refrigerator and removes a tray laden with fruit, cheese, and crackers. The bright colors are too cheerful for the tension-filled atmosphere. Like the black-and-white decor all around us, Hayden and I are complete opposites. While he's domi-neering and severe, I'm caring and tender-hearted.

In a perfect world, we'd complement one another.

In a fucked-up world, we'd devastate each other.

He places the food next to me, and I eye it dispassion-ately. I wasn't lying when I said it's difficult for me to eat when I'm stressed. Between losing my father and my recent financial situation, I'm thinner than I've ever been in my life. You'd never know it from the way Hayden stares at me.

Like he's doing now.

After reaching for a cracker and placing a slice of cheese on top, he offers it to me. I shake my head. Vigorously. Everything he does—except being a deceitful asshole—is sexy. I'll be damned before I let him seduce me with a fucking piece of cheese. Accepting anything from him would feel like an act of surrender.

"I can do it myself."

"I know."

"Hayden..." I warn.

"It's either this," he says, lifting the food, "or my cock. Your choice."

My jaw drops. He's quick to take advantage of my bewildered state and plops the cracker into my mouth. While giving him a death glare, I chew, silently appreciating the sharp flavor coating my tongue.

"Good girl," he murmurs.

I choke, my eyes widening. After forcing myself to swallow the food, I resume squinting at him. Hayden picks up a strawberry and bites into it slowly, his eyes never leaving mine. Juice drips down his long fingers, and my mouth goes dry at the memory of what he's done to me with them.

"My eyes are up here," he says in a lazy drawl.

Caught ogling him, I stiffen and avert my gaze. He's quick to place a finger under my chin and guide my head back toward him.

"Open for me," he says. When I part my lips, his pupils contract. "Such a good girl."

Heat sweeps through me at the praise. Arousal and anger combine, leaving me hot and shaky. I clench my thighs and focus my thoughts on anything except the man in front of me, but he keeps bringing my attention back to him with every touch and every spoken word.

I force myself to remain still until I've consumed a fair amount of food, and then I hop down before Hayden can stop me. After racing to the other side and putting the island between us, I shake my head.

"I'm full."

He sets down the piece of pineapple in his hand and reaches for a napkin to wipe his fingers. "Then it's time for bed."

"I'm not sleeping with you."

His head snaps up. "Care to repeat that?"

"Nope."

Amusement flickers in his eyes. "I didn't think so."

"I'm serious. I need time to think."

"You can. In my bed. With me."

I come close to stomping my foot like a petulant child. "You're not listening to me."

"I'm definitely hearing you. I'm just denying your suggestion."

"It isn't a suggestion or a request or anything that fucking requires permission."

"Language, Miss Green."

I let out an honest-to-goodness scream. The sound bounces off the walls and furniture, piercing my eardrums hard enough for me to stop. When I clamp my lips together, Hayden tilts his head.

"Feel better?" he asks, his tone chiding and unfazed.

"Not really."

"Come here."

It's not a request.

I eye him with suspicion. "Why?"

"You look exhausted."

"I've had a pretty exciting day." I don't bother hiding my sarcastic undertone. "How often does a girl find out that the man she's living with is her stalker?"

"How often does a man find a woman he'd destroy the world for?"

I bow my head and release a sigh of defeat while briefly closing my eyes, ignoring the way my heart lurches in my chest. "Stop. I can't do this with you right now."

"Come here, Callie."

His tone is soft and gentle, soothing to my wounded soul. I slap my palms against the island to keep from going to him. To keep from accepting the comfort of a monster.

"I need to be alone," I say, my voice small and weak. Every time I deny Hayden, it adds another crack to my defense against him. When he's domineering, I can patch the holes in my armor, but this tender side of him?

It wrecks me.

"Please." My supplication is a mere whisper, the last of my rebellion a monosyllable of both weakness and desperation.

Hayden stares at me from across the island, so close physically, but very distant emotionally. The chasm between us is a third party, a looming presence in our relationship. Whatever's left of it.

The beautiful man in front of me swallows hard, right before blowing out a harsh breath. "Very well."

I don't ask him what he means. Instead, I take the brief reprieve and edge around the island. And him. Once my feet meet the carpet, I head in the direction of the guest room located a few doors down from Hayden's bedroom.

My spine tingles the entire way and my senses strain to pick up on any trace of him following me. When I reach the hallway, I stop and chance a look over my shoulder.

Hayden's exactly where I left him in the kitchen. Tension lines his entire frame. He's completely still, but that's not what steals my breath. The man grips the countertop with his head bowed, his body in a position of defeat and utter despair.

I bite the inside of my cheek to refrain from calling him. Or worse, returning to his side. I might care for Hayden, but we won't resolve this issue between us unless he can see how his behavior hurt me.

It takes every ounce of my willpower to turn back around and take a step. Once I'm in motion, I pick up the pace until I'm in the empty bedroom with the door shut and locked behind me.

A grim smile twists my mouth as I lean heavily against the door. Hayden might get upset because I've secured myself inside the room, but he's left me no choice. I need a moment of peace.

Not that I believe a simple metal mechanism would keep him from getting to me. It certainly didn't work at my apartment.

With a groan, I slide down until my butt hits the floor. Bringing my knees to my chest, I rest my forehead on them and wrap my arms around my legs. Curled in a tight ball, I let the tears flow.

I cry over my battered heart.

I weep over my broken trust.

I mourn over my bleak future.

How am I supposed to move past Hayden's lies? Is that even possible? I have no idea. The frightful unknown mixes with agony to create an unbearable anxiety. My sobs grow more desperate. My entire body is nothing more than a collection of skin and bones held firmly together while I feel like I'm falling apart on the inside.

How can one person be responsible for so much pain?

My shuddering causes my spine to rap against the wooden surface behind me, the staccato tapping the sound-track of my misery. Every tremor and every tear, a manifestation of my bleeding heart that struggles to beat despite me drawing breath.

I can feel Hayden's presence before I hear him speak. "Baby?"

The term of endearment has my soul wailing. I bite down on my fist until the tang of blood hits my tongue.

I can't go to him, not when I'm the one who asked for space. But hearing his voice and the concern underlying it? I'm like an addict wanting a drug, knowing it'll just hurt me.

The charged silence becomes heavier with every second I refuse to speak. My sobs immediately quiet with Hayden standing on the other side of the door. I don't stifle them for his benefit. I do it for mine.

I won't give him a reason to break the lock or the remaining shreds of my dignity.

At the sound of his footsteps receding, I release a sigh of relief. I might've held my breath when there was a mere three inches between us, but my tears continued to stream down my face. Sometimes, I think they'll never stop. But like all things, they come to an end.

I lie down on the floor, uncaring about comfort or anything else while chasing the blissful reprieve found in sleep. Closing my eyes, I concentrate on my heartbeat instead of the man down the hall.

Except my brain refuses to cooperate. I might've told Hayden he'll never invade my mind, but I lied.

The man follows me into my dreams.

Turning them into nightmares.

CHAPTER 3

H ayden

THE ENTIRE DAY HAS BEEN ONE GIANT CLUSTERFUCK.

I grip the edge of the counter until my arms tremble and my muscles ache. This tiny bit of discomfort pales in comparison to the frustration coursing through me like molten lava, incinerating my insides with guilt. I want to rip this emotion from my chest, but no amount of violence will rid me of the unwelcome emotion.

My only hope for serenity lies in a woman who despises me.

I shove away from the island and walk into the living room. My thoughts are as scattered as the pearls all over the floor. I bend down to pick up the pieces of jewelry and curse myself for not being more careful to hide them. If I hadn't been so obsessed with finding Calista's assailant, then I wouldn't have forgotten the pearls in my coat.

In a manner of minutes, they're back in my pocket. *All*

sixty-four of them. I counted the total the night I broke into Calista's apartment. I wanted to know how many times it'd take to fuck myself before I was through giving them back to her. Turns out I didn't need that many.

I might now.

Of its own volition, my head swings in the direction she just left, my eyes hungry for a glimpse of her. The hallway is empty. My disappointment rises, along with my craving for her. After my discovery of the date-rape drug's connection to all three crimes, I wanted to ease my worries in the heat of her cunt and the warmth of her embrace, but the look she gave me when I walked in the door...

I shake my head as if that'll rid me of the mental image. In my mind's eye, Calista gazes at me with something worse than anger. The pain of betrayal. In that moment, I would've given anything to erase that hurt from her expression. Witnessing it was pure agony, but knowing I'm the reason for it?

Brutal.

I won't apologize for stalking her. If I did, it'd be a lie, and I've told her enough of those already. That doesn't mean I'm going to reveal the truth about her father's murder. If Calista thinks she hates me now, then knowing that will ruin any chance of me winning her heart.

I've probably already fucked up my chance with her.

But I won't give up. I can't, not when she's my reason for living. Before her, I simply existed. Now that I know what it feels like to receive her affection, I can never go back to the way things were before.

Revenge isn't enough.

Maybe it never was.

My need for justice still lingers. If anything, it's amplified because of Calista's history. The secretary's murder led to me killing Senator Green, which, in turn, ruined Calista's life. I'm going to make things right, no matter what or how long it takes.

The only thing stronger than my determination is my need for her.

I stare out of the window, my gaze tracing the city's skyline. The lights battle against the darkness of night and cast a glow on everything they touch. That's what Calista does for me. She sheds light on my dark soul.

A muffled tapping reaches my ears, and I tilt my head, concentrating on the noise. I straighten and follow the sound until I'm standing in front of the door to the guest bedroom, where I can clearly hear it.

Along with Calista's sobs.

They gut me, and I nearly double over. Instead, I remain completely still, unsure of what to do. Instinct demands that I break down the fucking door, but I can't give into my urges.

I can't listen to her suffering either.

I raise my hand to knock and end up letting it fall to my side. This might be my house, but right now, Calista holds all the power over this situation. Over *me*.

I inhale and slowly blow out the breath before calling to her. "Baby?"

The gently spoken word takes me by surprise. I'm aware I've said this term of endearment to her before, but using it right now is proof of my vulnerability when it comes to this woman. Does Calista know that she could ask for anything and I wouldn't have the strength to deny her if meant she'd come back to me?

I grit my teeth. Regardless of our disagreement, she belongs to me. I won't entertain the thought of anything else. It's simply not acceptable.

Being without her isn't an option for me.

Or for her.

It takes every ounce of willpower I possess to walk away from the sounds of her suffering. Once in the confines of my bedroom, I pace to ease the riotous emotions raging inside me. Calista's tear-filled eyes haunt me, and her sobs echo in my ears until I'm gripping my hair, ready to rip it from my scalp.

Things have to go back to the way they were. I can't imagine never seeing her smile or hearing her laughter again. When I first met Calista during her father's trial, I wanted to know everything about her. It wasn't until the senator's funeral that I finally gave myself permission to do so.

Calista has a goodness in her that the vileness of her trauma hasn't been able to kill. The purity of her heart is what I discovered and then sought to protect all those months ago. Nothing's changed. If that means deception, then so be it.

Her anger and hurt will fade in time. It has to. I acted with good intentions. My entire motivation was keeping her safe. Calista doesn't see it right now, but she will.

She has to.

I wait as long as I can before the urge to go to her is overwhelming. Then I'm striding back to her door with my lock picks in hand. My need to check on her outweighs her need for privacy. Once I know she's okay, I'll have the reassurance I need to walk away.

God, I'm so full of shit.

Calista's sleeping in my bed and nowhere else.

The entire penthouse is eerily quiet. There are no sobs or rhythmic tapping on the door. The only sound is the soft click of the lock sliding and the turning of the knob that engages the door's mechanism.

I pull it open and peer into the darkness. The moonlight illuminates the room, allowing me to make out the untouched bed and empty chair. With my pulse thumping in my ears, I quickly scan the area, my gaze landing at the woman curled up by my feet.

After dropping to a crouch, I place my fingers on her neck and breathe a sigh of relief at finding her pulse steady. Calista doesn't stir at my touch, the rise and fall of her chest continuing at an even pace.

She's beautiful when she sleeps.

I brush a loose strand of hair from her face, almost groaning at the feel of her skin. Touching her isn't just pleasurable to me. It's fucking therapeutic.

The turmoil within me begins to lessen the minute I scoop her into my arms. I wait for her to awaken and fight me, but she remains deep in slumber. Without her resistance, I cradle her to my chest and breathe in her scent, the floral perfume filling my senses.

I carry her to my room, my steps even to keep from jarring her awake. I like Calista when she's fiery, but tonight I need to hold her. If only to soothe my demons for a time.

When I reach my bed, a pang of reluctance runs through me at the idea of putting her down. I shake my head at myself and do it anyway with the intention to join her. Calista's place is by my side.

At all times.

The warmth of her skin lingers on my hands, and I curl them into fists to keep from touching her the way I want to. Instead, I carefully undress her. Beginning with her blouse, I undo the buttons until I reveal the soft mounds of her breasts and the graceful dip of her stomach. Every inch of skin tantalizes me.

Lust sweeps through me, as it always does at the sight of

this woman. I'm quick to shove it aside and continue removing her clothing. The jeans are a challenge, not only to take off without waking her, but when I catch sight of her lacy underwear, I nearly rip them from her body.

I may not be able to get inside Calista's head, but she's fucked with mine.

Once she's in nothing except her bra and underwear, I undress until I'm completely nude. There's no doubt in my mind that Calista's going to be pissed when she wakes up in my bed, so me being naked won't make a difference.

I ease onto the mattress and slide my arms around her, pulling her body flush to mine, her back to my chest. The physical contact puts me at ease, as does the gentle rhythm of her breathing. However, the tearstains on her cheek are like a knife twisting in my gut.

"You're mine," I say, reaching out to touch her, to temper the guilt that's rising again. I trail my fingers over her hair, along her shoulder, and down her arm until I reach the curve of her hip. "I won't let you leave," I whisper against her skin. "I warned you that I wanted to own you, and I do. Every single piece of you belongs to me now."

I pause for a moment when she sighs in her sleep. The sound is unguarded, trusting. It stirs something deep inside me, something I don't want to identify.

"Your capacity for forgiveness confuses me, but I need it," I say. "I'll never apologize for protecting you because your life is all that matters to me. However, I'm sorry for hurting you."

The sincerity of my words astounds me as much as the fact that I apologized, which is something I've never felt the need to do. But Calista is so much more than my lover. She's the woman I care for.

And my future wife.

CHAPTER 4

C alista

The dream-like state between sleeping and being awake is one of my favorite experiences. It's a small moment in time where my worries haven't plagued me and there's nothing except complete serenity. It's like a warm cocoon protecting me from the rest of the world.

As I slowly drift into wakefulness, that comfort threatens to slip away. I cling to it, trying to remain in this tranquil state for a little longer, but awareness creeps in. An unfamiliar weight draped over my side has my eyes fluttering open.

I scan the room, immediately noting it's Hayden's. Then memories from last night return to me in a rush. The pearls and his lies. The revealed truth and my tears.

Except I don't remember how I ended up in his bed.

My entire body tingles with alarm. I turn my head slightly and freeze. Hayden is curled against me with his arm wrapped around my waist, his face nuzzled into the curve of my shoulder. His breath whispers across my skin, warm and steady. Our legs are tangled underneath the sheets, and my flesh burns wherever his bare skin touches mine. Considering he's naked, I feel like I'm on fire.

Ignoring my body's reaction to his proximity, I stare at him. I've never seen Hayden this way, and I commit it to memory, unable to help myself. His features are smoothed by repose, his face lacking the harsh lines around his mouth, eyes, and forehead that give him a severe countenance. As well as a callous one.

This unguarded expression makes him appear approachable instead of aloof.

Lovable instead of hateful.

My heart stutters painfully in my chest. I know I should leave—not just his bed, but this entire relationship. Yet there's a part of me, a *very* foolish one, that wants this thing between us to work out.

My eyes drift shut as I'm lulled by his steady breathing and the warmth of his body pressed against mine. It doesn't take any effort to ignore my problems and concentrate on the man holding me in his arms as though he's afraid to lose me.

If he hasn't already...

I think back on our fight and shiver at the coldness that radiated from Hayden while he looked me in the eyes and admitted to being my stalker. Instead of apologizing and seeking forgiveness, he used my safety to justify his actions.

The brief moment of tranquility in his embrace fades with the rising of the sun. I turn back around, my fingers curling into fists around the sheets. Resentment wars with affection inside me until I think I might implode.

As if sensing my turmoil, Hayden stirs. He nuzzles my

shoulder and murmurs something I can't make out...except for a single word.

Baby.

My eyes sting with unshed tears, and the lump forming in my throat makes it difficult to breathe. I focus on keeping my shit together by pulling air into my lungs and blowing it back out slowly. He obliterates my efforts by tightening his arm around my waist, a contented sigh leaving his lips.

I'm trapped, pinned beneath him and under the weight of his betrayal. Not to mention my own shattered illusions of love and happiness.

Hayden's breath skims the curve of my neck, right before his entire frame goes rigid. He lifts his head, and I can feel his gaze sweeping over me. It's like a physical caress. I grit my teeth to remain unmoving, not wanting to show any reaction to him.

"Calista?" Threads of uncertainty underlie his tone despite the gruffness of sleep coating his voice. "Are you awake?"

I nod, not trusting myself to speak but knowing that if I ignore Hayden, I'll invite more issues into an already tenuous situation. There's no reason to play games with a man who refuses to obey the rules.

"Look at me." It's not a request. With Hayden, it rarely is.

"No," I say.

I unclench the sheets to slap a hand against his arm with the intention to shove him away. The second my palm makes contact with his forearm, Hayden moves. From one blink to the next, he flips me onto my back and then positions himself above me, his knees flanking my hips and his hands encircling my wrists on either side of my head.

The breath stills in my lungs at the feel of his body pressed to mine and because of the look on his face. I stare up at him, unsurprised by the anger I find there. It's the brief flicker of panic that I can't readily dismiss.

Hayden is quiet for a long while. When he speaks again, his voice is controlled, his expression stoic once more. "Calista, we need to talk."

I avert my gaze, both unwilling and unable to meet his.

"Just listen to me," he says, his fingers tightening on my wrists. "The drug someone gave you is the same one that was found in Kristen Hall's bloodstream, as well as the one that caused my mother's death. They're not individual cases like I originally thought. All of these events are connected."

My eyes dart to his as fear turns my blood to ice. I search his face for any signs of ambivalence, but there are none. When I open my mouth to respond with a weak denial, nothing comes out. Tears well up and spill down my temples.

Hayden makes a low, anguished sound before releasing one of my wrists to wipe away my tears. The show of tenderness only causes them to flow all the more. I squeeze my eyes shut against the swell of emotions threatening to drown me.

"This drug came from somewhere," he says, "and I won't stop until I uncover the creator, the manufacturer, and the distributors. All of this could be the key to closing these cases, or it could lead nowhere. Either way, I'll find out. I promise they won't get away with it."

Despite his aggressive tone, he grazes the inside of my wrist with gentle strokes of his thumb. I hold back a wince. Hayden's touch soothes my wounds even as he inflicts new ones with his nearness.

"Shh, Callie. It's all right."

He leans down to kiss my damp skin. The contact nearly undoes me. I stiffen at the feel of his lips, squeezing my eyes shut. The uncharacteristic show of affection warms my heart. Traitorous piece of shit.

"Don't worry," he whispers, his breath skimming my mouth. He places a kiss on my eyelids, one, then the other. "We'll get through this."

I let out a shaky exhale, comforted by his strength and confidence despite everything he's done. The pain isn't gone and my worries extend beyond this new information, but there's too much unresolved between us for me to think clearly.

"I need to leave," I say, finally gathering the courage to look at him.

He shakes his head.

"What do you want?"

"So many things, but I'll start with a promise from you."

I frown. "What do you mean?"

"I want you to promise not to run away. I know you think I'm—"

"You don't know anything," I say, my voice rising in volume. "I trusted you, and you lied to me, Hayden."

"To keep you alive!" His shout echoes in the bedroom, startling me into silence. "Don't you get it? If I lose you, Callie, I won't fucking survive it."

His outburst hangs in the air between us, raw and full of anguish. I stare up at him, watching the torment illuminate his eyes, turning them into gems. He drags a hand over his face and blows out a harsh breath.

"You're right," he says. "I don't know a damn thing anymore, not when it comes to you."

"Hayden, I..."

He slides his hand through my hair to grip the nape of my neck. With a firm jerk, he tilts my head back, forcing me to meet his gaze. "You're not leaving this bed until you agree to let me keep you safe," he says. "You can hate me, but you'll give me what I want."

I press my lips together, unwilling to commit to anything without thinking it through. Not running means having to be near him every day, and, to an extent, trusting him not to hurt me further. That's a significant promise to make.

And risk to take.

Hayden releases my wrists to caress my hip. My thoughts slip away like grains of sand in an ocean wave. I blink several times to regain my focus while he looks down at me, his eyes glinting with determination and desire.

Persuasion through seduction.

Is there anything deadlier?

I want to arch into his touch, to melt into him until I forget his deception and there's nothing between us except pleasure. It takes every ounce of willpower I have to stay still, but that doesn't stop my body from reacting to him. Heat ignites wherever his fingers graze my skin. My breathing hitches, and my breasts get heavy, my nipples hardening, begging for his mouth.

His need for my submission is written all over his face, in every bit of tension lining his body. He shifts above me to dip his hand between my thighs. My breath leaves me in a rush at the feel of his thumb brushing my clit through my panties.

He lowers his head to nip at my earlobe before running his tongue along the shell of my ear. "I'll wait as long as it takes."

I place my hands on his chest, and the muscles underneath twitch at my touch. He's just as affected by me as I am by him. This isn't a revelation, but it does empower me.

"I want something first," I say.

He lifts his head, his brow furrowing in skepticism.

"You're in no position to negotiate. Unless you're using your body as collateral?"

He yanks the crotch of my panties to the side and thrusts two fingers in me. A moan slips from me, filling the space between us. I dig my nails into his chest to keep from lifting my hips and taking him deeper.

The side of Hayden's mouth lifts into a smirk. "Miss Green, would you care to explain how I was able to easily slide my fingers into this tight pussy of yours?"

I shake my head.

"It's because you're so fucking wet," he says. "You might think you hate me, but your body tells me otherwise."

"Hayden." My voice is breathy, lacking the conviction I need when dealing with this man. "Don't."

"Don't what?" He curls his fingers, causing pleasure to skitter through me. "Don't...stop? Tell me what you want, Callie."

He begins to stroke me. My pride battles my passion. I soften underneath him, and a whimper dances on my tongue. I know the second he hears it. His movements increase in speed, with so much force that they lift my hips.

"Promise me," he says.

"I want something too."

"This isn't enough for you?" He inserts a third finger inside me, stretching me. When I gasp from the pleasure of it, he smiles. "Maybe you want my cock instead?"

"No," I lie. "I want you to pay for my education when I go back to college."

"Done."

I slam my thighs closed, but it doesn't stop him. If anything, he's rougher, more insistent on making me come. "I want a full ride, Hayden."

He smirks at me. "Absolutely."

A groan leaves me at his innuendo. I don't have the strength to fight him on this while he's fucking me with his fingers. "To Columbia." When he nods, I choke out, "Okay, I promise."

His eyes blaze with triumph and hunger. He slams his mouth to mine in a searing kiss as his fingers relentlessly drive me toward the edge. Rational thought is long gone, replaced by Hayden and my need for him. My orgasm hits me after I surrender to my body's demands, and I shatter in his arms. He holds me close, watching me with an intensity that borders on manic.

"Never argue with an attorney. You won't win."

CHAPTER 5

C alista

My self-control is non-existent when it comes to Hayden.

With one final look at the man responsible for my lack of restraint, I roll away from him and slip from the bed. He watches me as I walk to the closet, select an outfit, and head to the bathroom to get ready for the day.

"Where are you going, Calista?"

My spine stiffens at the sound of his voice, and I halt in my tracks. I remain frozen, unable to look at him when I respond. Hayden has a way of reading me that I find unpleasant, and it puts me at a disadvantage when it comes to dealing with him. "I have a doctor's appointment this morning."

"For what?"

"It's personal." I turn to glance at him over my shoulder. "For once, stay out of my business."

He scoffs. "You are my business. *Everything* about you. Especially your well-being."

"You're bad for my health. Just so you know."

His lips twitch. "Quit stalling."

"I'm going to see my OB-GYN."

He stares at me with a stricken look on his face and his eyes wide. Then they narrow with suspicion. "Are you trying to get rid of a pregnancy?"

I clutch my clothes to my chest and spin to face him. "Oh, my God. Are you serious?"

Hayden rises from the mattress, standing tall with his arms crossed. The sunlight hits his body, turning it golden. Every divot and sinew of muscle is on display for me to gaze at like a Roman statue. Only he's flesh and blood, and a temptation I can't give into. Not again.

"Answer the question," he says, the words measured but forceful.

"That's not the reason for my appointment."

"Then what is?"

I sigh. "Birth control, okay? My blood pressure is probably through the roof because of this conversation," I mutter.

His stance relaxes, and his arms fall to his sides, completely at odds with the urgency in his tone. "Would you tell me if you were pregnant, Callie?"

I frown. "Of course. You'd have a right to know."

He nods, coming to an unspoken conclusion. "So, birth control, huh?"

"Yes."

A smile spreads his lips. "Why do you need it?"

"Why do I need it?" My forehead scrunches with my confusion. "What are you getting at, Hayden? And why do you have that stupid grin on your face?"

"You wouldn't need birth control unless you were still planning on having sex with me."

A loud huff leaves me before I purse my lips. "I made the appointment *before* I found out about your...nocturnal activities in my apartment."

"That's fair," he says, dipping his head in a show of agreement, "but the fact that you're *still* going to the appointment tells me what I want to know."

"I'm going to regret asking this, but what does your twisted mind tell you? That I don't want to get knocked up by a psychopath?"

"That you want to forgive me."

My pulse hammers loudly in my ears until it drowns out everything else. I stare at Hayden, waiting for anger or denial to rise within me, but nothing happens. Nothing except feelings of helplessness pricking at me.

And a tinge of suspicion that he could be right...

"This is too much," I say. I grip the clothing harder to hide the trembling of my fingers, wrinkling the garments. "And it's not that simple."

His jaw tightens. "Maybe not, but the inclination is there."

"Go to hell."

He laughs to himself, the sound hollow and forlorn. "Go to hell? Without you, I'm already there."

AFTER WAITING SEVERAL MINUTES FOR HAYDEN TO FORCE HIS way into the bathroom, I finally relax when he doesn't appear. I go through my morning routine methodically, but not because I care about my appearance. It's about focusing on the tasks rather than my conflicted emotions.

Once I'm showered and dressed with my hair and makeup done, I study my reflection. The woman staring back at me is calm and collected, but she has dark circles under her eyes. No amount of concealer can disguise that.

Just as no amount of denial can erase the pleasure I experienced in Hayden's arms this morning.

Pushing that thought aside, I grab my purse and make my way to the kitchen. Hayden is there, freshly showered and fully dressed. His gaze locks on me the second I appear and doesn't waver, even when I glare at him in suspicion.

He juts his chin at the travel mug on the counter. "Take it."

"Thank you."

"What type of contraceptive are you going to request?"

I avert my gaze, becoming self-conscious at the question. "Does it matter?"

"How many times do I have to tell you? Everything about you matters to me."

"I'm thinking about getting the shot." When he remains quiet, I look up at him. "Does that meet your approval, Mr. Bennett?"

He lifts a brow. "Nothing short of you being pregnant meets my approval, Miss Green."

"You don't mean that."

"Don't I?"

I search his face, finding nothing except complete resolution. "Hayden..."

"You don't have to say anything."

"There's nothing to say."

He braces himself against the granite counter and leans back. "Maybe, but that doesn't mean I haven't thought about it."

I stare at him as if meeting him for the first time. "I had no idea you wanted to be a father."

"I didn't until I met you."

A blush works its way onto my cheeks while I tuck a strand of hair behind my ear, ignoring my fluttering heart. "Oh."

"What's the name of your doctor?"

"I'm going to the clinic on 4th and Stanton."

His eyes widen. "The one for low-income patients?"

"Yes." I plant my hands on my hips. "I couldn't afford health insurance when I made the appointment, but that'll change once the enrollment period opens up again."

He shakes his head vehemently. "You're going to a physician of my choosing, not some run-down clinic in a shitty part of town."

I open my mouth to protest, but after one phone call, Hayden arranges an appointment for me at the exact same time as my old one. "Dr. Sheridan comes highly recommended," he says. "She'll be happy to have you as a new patient this morning."

After throwing up my hands in defeat, I nod. I'll never admit it to Hayden, but I'm relieved to avoid the rougher neighborhoods of the city. "Fine, but I have to leave now, or I'll be late."

Hayden slowly nods, reluctance covering his features. "Sebastian will go with you."

"I assumed so. Besides, I've gotten used to him being my shadow." I shrug. "As long as he's not inside the exam room, I don't care."

"If Sebastian's in the exam room, he and I will have a *private* conversation afterwards."

I don't doubt it.

"I don't want to know," I mutter.

Hayden pushes away from the counter and walks over to me. I hold my ground by locking my knees instead of taking a retreating step back, like my instincts demand. He stops directly in front of me, close enough for my breasts to press against his chest and the heat of his body to warm me.

His gaze searches mine, a silent plea in their depths, before he leans down to press a kiss to my forehead. I savor the brief moment of tenderness, my eyes drifting shut.

"Be safe," he murmurs, his voice quiet yet strained with want.

I open my eyes to find him watching me closely. "How did I end up in your bed last night?"

Hayden's mouth thins. He remains silent for a time, as if carefully choosing his words. Or because he's hesitating.

"I needed you there."

His confession unsettles me, throwing my emotions into chaos. I stand there, trying to reconcile this vulnerability with the domineering man I know. "Hayden, I..."

He flicks his gaze to my lips in wordless longing. "If you don't leave right now, I'm going to kiss you like I've wanted to do since you walked in here. And I won't stop until I've finished what I started this morning."

He raises his gaze to mine, giving me an unobstructed view of the yearning within. The draw between us is undeniable, a palpable tension in the room. But I can't give in to him again. Not with my appointment looming and my pride still wounded.

"I'll see you later," I say quietly.

Hayden simply inclines his head, his expression now shuttered. With a final glance at him, I walk toward the door, feeling his gaze on me the entire way. Only when I'm out in the hallway am I released from his presence. Clearing my mind, I center my thoughts on the reason for my appointment.

I knew from the beginning that I needed to be responsible and get on birth control. Hayden and I have been reckless in our passion so far. Or at least I have. He had the good sense to pull out before coming inside me. I'm the one who wasn't thinking of consequences, but I am now.

If Hayden wanted to possess me before we had sex, how would he be if I got pregnant with his child?

I can't even begin to imagine. An unplanned pregnancy would ruin my already fractured relationship with Hayden, despite what he thinks. Seeing as he's determined to stay and I can't get rid of him, I'm going to concentrate on taking care of myself by obtaining a pregnancy test and some birth control.

I walk up to Sebastian as soon as I spot him in the lobby. He nods at me when our eyes meet. I lift my chin, refusing to be intimidated, even if this man could break my neck like a twig.

"Good morning, Sebastian."

"Good morning, Mrs. Bennett."

My mouth falls open. It takes me several moments to gather my composure and once I do, I snap my jaws closed, making my teeth click. "I'm sorry. What'd you say?"

"Is there a problem?"

"Yes. My name is *Miss Green*."

He shrugs his massive shoulders. "I have my orders from Mr. Bennett to address you as such."

"But—"

"I'm sorry, but you'll have to discuss it with him."

I squint up at him. "Oh, I'm planning on it."

CHAPTER 6

C alista

"THERE SHE IS!"

Harper's smile is as welcoming as her voice. And just as obnoxious.

"Hey." A grin works its way onto my mouth despite the last twenty-four hours having stripped me of my newfound happiness. "How's it going?"

"I like working with Alex, but he's not my bestie. I'm glad I get to see you before my shift ends."

"Me too."

Harper flicks her gaze over my shoulder, her expression full of intrigue. "Who's the muscle?"

I sigh. "My bodyguard, courtesy of Hayden."

"God, that man is crazy." She winks at me. "I mean crazy for you, of course."

"Oh, he's definitely a psycho."

I walk over to put away my purse and then retrieve my

apron. The redhead trails me closer than Sebastian would ever dare. "You have a look on your face. I need to know everything," Harper says, her voice quivering with excitement. "Did he spank you? Tie you up? You know I'm a Shibari expert. If you really want to escape, I can help with that. But why would you? Am I right?"

She waggles her eyebrows at me, and I roll my eyes at her. "It's nothing like that," I say. Although I wish it was.

"Then what?" Harper runs her gaze over me in a silent assessment before pinning me with her stare. "Where were you this morning?"

"I was at the doctor's."

Her green eyes grow clouded with worry. "Are you sick?"

"No." I scan the room for Alex and lower my voice. "I got on birth control."

"Smart move. You don't want to have little Calista baristas running around. That'd put a stop to your sex life faster than being an extra dick at a porno shoot."

"Agreed."

I walk up to the counter and open the till. The bills are all facing different directions, just like I anticipated. I rearrange the money, glad for something to keep my mind occupied until a customer walks in.

Harper bumps me with her hip and leans against the counter, folding her arms. "What's wrong?"

"Would you ever lie to someone to keep them safe?"

Harper scoffs. "Duh."

I jerk my head up to look at her. "What about breaking trust?"

"How serious are we talking about? Is it a life-or-death situation?" When I give her a reluctant nod, she shrugs. "Trust doesn't matter if they're dead. Personally, I wouldn't get caught lying in the first place. But *if* I did, then I'd take whatever they dish out. It's hard to stay mad at someone who has your best interests at heart."

"Unbelievable."

I close the register and reach for the sanitizer, pumping it like it's a whack-a-mole. Or Hayden's face. I rub the liquid all over my hands, and Harper watches me the entire time.

"Your silence scares me," I mutter. "Say something, or I'll sic Sebastian on you."

She looks over at the bodyguard sitting on the far side of the coffee shop and blows him a kiss before turning to look at me. "Don't threaten me with a good time. His tattoos are sexy as shit."

"Do you see the one on his neck?" I whisper. "I think it means he's part of the *Bratva*, the Russian mob."

Now Harper's rubbing her hands together like she's the one using hand sanitizer. "Bring on the big boy. I'd buff that bald head of his until it shines. And the one on his shoulders too."

I groan. "Please stop."

"I'll stop when you tell me what's wrong with you." She jabs her chest with her thumb. "Best friend, remember?"

"I know, but I can't talk about it. At least not until I've processed everything, okay?"

She sighs. "Fine. You've pretty much told me already with your *hypothetical* question. I'll do my best to wait for the rest of the details."

"Thank you."

"Listen," she says, gripping my shoulders. "Your boyfriend is...unconventional, which means his methods are going to be as well. That man deals in extremes. Hot or cold, life or death, love or hate. If you told me he was on an even keel now that you're together, I'd say you were full of shit. That man doesn't know how to be normal. He's going to give you everything. You just have to decide if you can handle all of him."

My eyes burn, and I blink rapidly to avoid any tears. "What if I can't?"

"That's your choice to make. But that's not the only issue." When I press my lips together, Harper squeezes my shoulders in a show of comfort. "If that man gives you everything, he's going to want everything in return. And I mean *everything*."

"I know."

She releases me to greet a customer while I stand there in a daze. What if I'm not scared of being in Hayden's life but frightened at the idea of him invading every part of mine? I don't have anything to hide. However, that doesn't mean I want to relinquish my control completely in order to be with him.

That's what he wants.

It might be what he's always wanted.

The door to the Sugar Cube opens, and I swing my gaze to find a delivery man striding inside. The blonde nods at me, but when he catches sight of Harper, he smiles, showing his teeth. "I have a delivery for a Calista Green," he says.

I catch Sebastian shifting in his seat at the announcement, and I shake my head at him. "That's me," I tell the newcomer.

"Ooh, a package." Harper sidles up to me with an espresso in hand. She offers it to the delivery guy with a playful pout. "It's not a big package. How disappointing."

He sets the box on the counter and leans forward to take the coffee from her. "This isn't the only package I can deliver."

"Why didn't you say so, handsome?"

I slide the plain brown box closer, interrupting them

before Sebastian decides to come over here. "Do you have a pen I can borrow?"

"That should've been my line," Harper mutters.

"Sign here please," the delivery man says, handing me an electronic pad.

I take the device from him and scribble my name. "Thank you."

"Have a good day, handsome." Harper waves. "I hope you have a package for me next time."

The man winks at her and Harper's cheeks turn as red as her hair. "I definitely will, beautiful."

I drop my gaze to the box that's no more than six inches in length. It's just my name printed on the front, without a return address, and it weighs next to nothing.

"What did Mr. Tall-dark-and-dangerous-dick-size Bennett get you?" Harper asks once we're alone. She swipes the box from my hands. "Is it a gift or an apology?"

"I doubt it. Hayden doesn't think he's wrong in the first place."

"That doesn't mean you won't like what's inside. Mind if I open it?"

I wave a hand. "It's fine. I doubt there's anything that'll get me to change my mind."

Harper tears into the paper, stripping it away like a T. rex, her arms a flurry of movement. She peels back the pink tissue paper inside with her lips forming an "O."

"These are sexy," she says, holding up black underwear. "Why isn't there a matching bra? I'm disappointed. You'd think the attorney would know how to present a case."

I stare at the panties—*my* panties—the ones that went missing the night I was assaulted in the children's shelter.

The coffee shop fades from view as my entire focus centers on the scrap of lace in Harper's fingers. My thoughts spiral, one following the other in rapid succession until my temples throb and my breathing thins.

Who sent this?

It has to be the person who took them.

"Oh, look," Harper says, her voice fuzzy to my ears. "There's a note inside. It says, 'Will wett ink ken?' Huh, that's weird. Not to mention the most un-sexy thing I've ever read. I can't believe..."

Her voice fades amidst the pounding in my head. Is that my heart struggling to beat? Or has it stopped due to the horror streaming through me, invading every inch of skin and every drop of blood?

"Calista, are you okay?"

Harper's face appears in my line of sight, but I stare straight ahead until her face becomes a blur. Then, my eyelids flutter shut, blackness takes over, and I can't see anything.

Even in the deep recess of my mind, the terror follows me.

CHAPTER 7

C alista

A SCREAM PIERCES MY SKULL LIKE AN ICE PICK.

Then Harper's voice penetrates my consciousness, as does the pain radiating along my shoulder. "Oh, my God, Calista!"

"Don't touch her." The deep boom of Sebastian's command has me opening my eyes. The bodyguard crouches over me while holding out his arm to block Harper. "If Mrs. Bennett has sustained a head injury, we can't move her."

"Mrs. *What*?" My friend shakes her head. "Never mind. What do we do now?"

"The ambulance is on the way. Get the customers out of here, and don't let anyone else in until we're gone. This situation needs to be handled with discretion."

Both Harper and Alex race to follow his orders while I blink against the overhead lights, trying to make sense of everything. My brain offers me nothing by way of explanation. The only thing I can concentrate on is the painful throbbing in my shoulder.

"What the hell happened?" Alex asks, coming to stand beside my bodyguard.

Harper takes up the spot on the other side of Sebastian, her face damp with tears. "Calista fainted and fell into the display case."

I scrunch my face in confusion, searching my mind once again for any memory of what just happened. Everything is blank except the image of the lacy panties. A surge of panic hits me, and I struggle to rise, my body urging me to take flight.

"The box...the note..."

Sebastian lays his hand on my chest, his touch gentle but firm. "Don't move. I don't think you have a concussion, but that's for the doctor to determine. Until then, lie still." A wry smile twists his thin lips. "Knowing Mr. Bennett, he'll be here before the ambulance is."

Harper straightens, her expression grim. "I can't sit here and do nothing while we're waiting. I'm going to sweep up the glass."

When I try to turn my head, Sebastian lifts his hand from my chest to rest it on the side of my face. "If you move you'll cut yourself. There's broken glass all around you. Don't worry though. Everything's going to be fine, Mrs. Bennett."

"Calista," I whisper.

He presses his lips together before giving me a nod. "I need you to stay calm, Calista."

"Okay."

The coffee shop, once a place of productivity, has transformed into a den of chaos. Not more than my mind. The reality of what happened sinks in, the way it affected me, to the point I had no control over my body and am now lying on the cool tile, surrounded by people concerned with my well-being.

Harper leans the broom against the counter with sweat dotting her forehead. "I've cleaned as much as I could without sweeping up Calista too." She smiles at me, but her lips tremble. When I attempt to smile in return, she wipes at her eyes.

The sound of someone pounding on the door startles me. Sebastian frowns while Harper rushes from behind the counter to let Hayden in. I watch him through the display case as he bursts through the door, his gaze widening when he takes in the destruction.

"Calista?!"

My heart lurches in my chest at the sound of his voice. It's frantic and unhinged. I mouth his name, unable to find my voice.

After a few strides, he rounds the counter, his face unreadable. However, his hair is tousled and there are deep wrinkles in his suit. Did he run to get here?

I stare up at him, taking in his blank expression and the way he clenches his fists, as if he doesn't want to touch me. Hayden might've rushed to my side, but he's not here to comfort me.

"What the fuck happened?" he asks.

A siren wails in the distance, growing louder every second, but all I can hear is Hayden's anger. Is he upset because I interrupted him at work? Given how much this man wants to possess me, he could be mad because I broke his favorite toy.

Me.

Sebastian lifts his gaze to Hayden, his expression calm.

"Mr. Bennett, she had a panic attack and fainted. From what I can tell, she doesn't have a concussion."

"And the blood?" Hayden asks.

"It has to be a laceration from the glass. I haven't moved her to ascertain the extent of the injury. My guess is it's superficial." When Hayden steps closer, Sebastian raises a hand. "Mr. Bennett, please stay back. The ambulance is almost here."

Hayden's entire body goes taut. "Remember who you work for."

"That's why I'm looking after her."

I flinch at the look Hayden gives him. Sebastian merely waits, holding his ground until the paramedics rush in. Once they do, Harper, Alex, and Sebastian step aside, their focus on me. Hayden doesn't move. He simply stares at the health professionals as if daring them to question his presence.

The paramedics begin to assess my condition, asking me a barrage of questions that I struggle to answer through a haze of pain and shock. Hayden remains by my side. I'd be comforted by him if he didn't look ready to unleash violence on someone.

I grit my teeth when I'm rolled onto my side and pain shoots through my shoulder. The new position allows me to see the blood that pooled underneath my back while I lay on the floor. Nausea rises, causing my stomach to lurch as I fight the urge to vomit.

For the second time that day, everything goes black.

A STEADY BEEPING CREEPS INTO MY CONSCIOUSNESS, WAKING ME.

I clench my teeth in irritation, ready to smash my alarm

clock into silence, but the sound of Hayden's voice keeps me still.

"Josephine, clear my schedule for the rest of the day." He pauses, and then, "Yes, Calista's fine, but I won't leave her for anything except court tomorrow."

I peek at him from underneath my lashes, unwilling to expose the fact that I'm eavesdropping. This man is brutally honest—more than I'm comfortable with on occasion—but he doesn't always tell me the things I'm desperate to hear. Right now, I'm aware of the depth of his concern for me. Considering he hasn't shown me an ounce of tenderness since he walked into the Sugar Cube, it's a nice change of pace.

"I'll be in the office tomorrow to prepare for Monroe's case," he says. "After that's done, I'll begin my emergency leave of absence. Make sure the paperwork for that is on Peter's desk today."

With my mind still fuzzy and my limbs heavy, it's not difficult for me to keep my facial features relaxed, but if it wasn't for that, my curiosity would give me away. An emergency leave of absence? My injuries aren't severe enough for that, so what's going on with Hayden? Is someone he cares about in trouble? He's never mentioned any siblings, but that doesn't mean he doesn't have them.

There's so much about this man that I don't know. While having insight into someone's past isn't a prerequisite to caring about them, it'd help when contemplating if you want to make them part of your future. I haven't decided what I'm going to do about Hayden, but I know for certain that he's decided to keep me.

I inhale slowly to remain calm, and the sterile scent of a hospital tickles my nose. The only sources of illumination in the private room are the few rays of sunshine peeking around the thick curtains and the neon lights on the machine next to my bed. Then there's Hayden's presence, looming like a specter, ready to possess me.

He ends the call with his secretary and dials another number. The phone rings twice before someone answers. I can't hear what he's saying, but the man's voice is young, light, and carefree.

"Zack, I need you to look into something for me immediately." Hayden's tone is dark and weighted with his urgency, the complete opposite of Zack's. "Calista received a package today while at work, and it triggered her. I want to know who sent it and why. There was a cryptic message inside, along with the underwear. I'm having everything sent to you. It'll be there within the hour."

Hayden runs his hand through his already disheveled hair. "I haven't asked her yet, but when I do, I'll call you. She's resting, so it'll have to wait." He flicks his gaze to me, giving me a clear view of the turmoil churning within. "For now, check the surveillance footage from the Sugar Cube, track down the delivery person, and dig into anything else that might give us a clue who's behind this. Revisit all of the information we have on her father and see if any of it's relevant. I don't care what else you've got on your plate. Make this your only priority."

I watch Hayden pocket his phone before he closes his eyes, his jaw tight and his hands fisted. As much as I want to call out to him, I can't. Just hearing about the delivery has my body tensing with panic.

The machine beeps loudly, revealing my elevated heart rate and snagging Hayden's attention. He sweeps his gaze over me as he walks to the side of the bed. I give up the pretense of sleeping and open my eyes fully. I lean forward to sit up straight, but he stays me with a hand on my forearm.

"Easy, Callie. Don't move just yet." When he withdraws his arm, I bite the inside of my cheek to keep from holding on to him. That contact, although brief, was enough to calm my racing heart. "How are you feeling?" he asks.

I look up at him, noting the dull ache in my back, as well as the bandage along my shoulder. Thankfully, the machine has stopped chiming. "Fine," I say, my voice cracking from disuse. I clear my throat and try again. "I'm fine."

"Are you in any pain?"

"Not really. I'm pretty groggy, though."

"It's the medication. You needed a few stitches, but you're not suffering from any serious head injuries."

I nod, unsure of what to say or how to act around him. Last night, I found out Hayden was my stalker, and it broke me. Today, I received a package that sent me into a panic attack that ended with me in the hospital. The more recent event doesn't lessen Hayden's guilt, but I can't deny it pales in comparison now. Especially when he's doing everything he can to figure out why this happened.

Part of me wants to thank him for taking the initiative, while the other part withers at the idea of him discussing this with me. I never want to relive the night of my assault, but with the look on his face, Hayden's not going to let this go. Even if he doesn't ask me about the panties right now, he will eventually.

"They're mine."

CHAPTER 8

C alista

My whispered confession sounds loud in the quiet. I bow my head as mortification drapes over me, weighing me down. "The panties in the box are mine."

Hayden settles on the bed next to me, and the scent of his cologne wafts under my nose. I want to breathe him in, but I don't. He takes my hand in his, refocusing my thoughts by gently sweeping his thumb over my skin in a soothing caress.

"You haven't done anything wrong, so why do you sound guilty?" he asks.

"I'm not. I'm ashamed."

"Why?"

I squint at him and yank my hand to remove it from his hold, but he tightens his grip until I give up. "I was wearing them on June 24th, and when I woke up drugged, I wasn't anymore. I haven't seen them since that night. Now do you get it?"

"Yes, I do."

The fury lacing his response has my fingers twitching. "Don't make me talk about it anymore."

"And the note?"

"I have no idea who sent it or what it means." I close my eyes, unable to look at him when I say, "I'm really tired. Please leave me alone."

He takes a deep breath as though to remain in control of his temper. "I'm not leaving you. Not now, not ever. When I told you that you're mine, I meant it. You're mine to protect, to care for, and to avenge. I won't ask for your permission, but things would be easier if you'd stop fighting me."

I look at Hayden, really study him. From the stubborn set of his jaw to the narrowing of his eyes, this man is determined to be in my life, even if it's by force of will. *My* will.

His refusal to leave should upset me, but the truth is I need him. As much as his presence overwhelms me, it comforts me more.

"You're obviously upset, and not just with me," he says. "What happened to you today was complete bullshit, and I understand that you're scared, but I promise I'll do everything in my power to resolve this. You may not trust me, but you can trust in that."

"I do."

"Good."

A knock on the door has Hayden straightening and both of us turning our heads. Harper comes into view, her steps purposeful and her face crestfallen.

"Oh, Calista," she cries.

My friend is by my side in an instant. Then she turns to

Hayden with her hands on her hips and glares at him. "Scoot over. It's my turn with her."

My eyes widen when he simply dips his head in acknowledgment before rising from the bed. Harper is quick to take his spot and grabs my hands, squeezing them gently.

"I'll be right outside," he says.

As soon as he's gone, Harper sniffles, bringing my attention back to her. "Are you okay?"

"Other than being a tiny bit sore, I'm fine."

"Oh, good. I was so worried. All of the glass and blood..." She swallows. "Today was shitty. That's all I'm saying."

I nod. "It's better now that you're here. Thank you for coming."

"Of course," she says with a scoff. "We're best friends. And since I hold that honorary title, do you want to tell me what really happened? I know it wasn't because your blood sugar dropped or some other medical issue."

"If I tell you, can you promise me to keep it a secret?"

Harper reaches out to tuck a stray curl behind my ear. "You're my ride or die, my bestie boo, my OG for infinity. I'll never betray you."

"Even if it's to keep me safe?"

"Is it really a betrayal if my motives have your best interests at heart?"

I groan and flop onto the pillow. "Why do you have to be so..."

"Sexy? Brilliant? Talented? I could go on all day."

"Annoying," I say with a smile.

"Don't be hateful just because I'm taking Hayden's side in whatever argument you guys are having. Don't think I haven't noticed. You're more depressed than Eeyore from

Winnie the Pooh, but your issue with him isn't what landed you in this hospital bed."

I blow out a breath. "I know."

"Are you going to trust me enough to tell me now?"

"Yes. Don't interrupt me, or I might not be able to get it all out."

"I want to help you, even if that means simply sitting here quietly."

I make a face. "Is that possible?"

"We're about to find out."

Before I can change my mind, I tell Harper about the night of my assault, Hayden's reaction, and his mission to find out everything and put an end to it. I don't admit to him being my stalker, but I do reveal the details of his behavior at the T&A, as well as him following me at night to and from my apartment. Knowing Harper, she'll make the connection on her own, and if she doesn't, that's fine with me.

My friend sits there without moving or speaking, but her eyes fill with tears, and she grips my hands tighter with every bit of revelation. By the end, I almost wish she were her usual self instead of stunned into silence.

"Now you know," I say.

"Now I know."

"Aren't you going to say something?"

Harper closes her eyes shut, and a tear leaks out. "You can be Eeyore if you want."

My chest squeezes in on itself. "As long as you'll be my Tigger. We both can't be sad."

"You're right." She wipes her face and straightens her shoulders. "Hayden is a demented Christopher Robin, and you'll be your normal Piglet self in no time."

"Rude."

"Okay, fine. You can be Kanga. She's sweet and nurturing." She gives me a pointed look. "Listen, you can deny it all you want, but at the end of the day, that man acts like his world revolves around you. Is it a little on the unhealthy side? Sure. But if I thought for one second that he'd hurt you, I'd kill him."

"The two of you are so...violent."

"Some things, or people, are worth it."

At the sound of the door opening, we shift our attention to the nurse walking inside. "Hello, Miss Green," she says.

"Thank you for trusting me." Harper jumps down from the bed and leans over to plant a kiss on my cheek. "Don't bust a stitch tonight."

"Huh?" I peer around the nurse to gape at my friend. "What are you talking about?"

She winks at me. "TTFN. Ta-ta for now."

CHAPTER 9

H ayden

I start to breathe easier once I have Calista behind the locked door of my penthouse.

Although I'm not sure the ache in my chest will ever subside, not after seeing her lying motionless in a pool of her own blood. I thought my worst nightmare brought to life was finding my mother's lifeless body, but that pales in comparison to Calista being in her place.

The visual is etched into my mind like a scar, ugly and permanent. I can't stop the shudder that runs through me. The show of weakness grates on my nerves, but it's a physical response to my need for her.

She frowns at me. "Are you okay?"

With someone threatening her, I'm far from okay. I'm close to losing my fucking mind.

I meet her gaze, exuding a fictitious calm to keep her

unaware of the thoughts torturing me. "I'm fine. Did you get enough to eat?"

She nods at the plate in front of her, still half-full. "Yes, thank you for dinner."

"You're welcome."

Silence descends on the room while the tension between us crescendos, the strains of yearning vibrating along my skin like a plucked violin string. I drum my fingers on the table to rid myself of the urge to touch her. It's pointless.

"I know you slept at the hospital, but it's getting late," I say. "Do you want to go to bed now?"

"Yes." Despite her blank expression, her voice holds a weariness that only exacerbates my desire to hold her. "I think I need to lie down," she says, "even if I don't fall asleep right away."

"Do you need another dose of your pain meds?"

She shakes her head. "My shoulder doesn't hurt at all."

I rise from my seat, flicking my gaze from her unfinished meal to the dark circles under her eyes. Despite her dramatic ordeal and obvious exhaustion, Calista sits with her back straight and her chin held high. My admiration for her fortitude swells.

As I turn to assist her, the scent of her fills my senses, reminding me of this morning when the smell of her pussy coated my fingers. She looks up at me, her hazel eyes studying me intently. In that tiny pause, I detect the hesitation that rises before she places her hand in mine, nervousness simmering beneath the surface of her skin.

She's right to worry. It's going to take everything I have not to fuck her tonight.

After pulling Calista to her feet, I immediately release her to avoid doing something I might regret. Actually, *I* wouldn't regret kissing her, but if her behavior is any indication, she'd take exception to it.

This is going to be a long fucking night.

This woman doesn't understand the hold she has on me. One glance, one touch, and I'd be on my knees for her. The realization is disturbing.

Calista runs her palms down her thighs and I stay silent, giving her time to compose herself. When she finally meets my gaze, she offers me a weak smile that wobbles on her lips. My fingers twitch with the need to soothe her, and I fist them at my sides.

With a curt nod, I gesture toward the hallway. "I'll escort you to your room."

"Thank you."

She walks beside me as I guide her by resting my hand on the small of her back. It's not enough to satiate my hunger. Each step is a dance, an opportunity for me to follow her lead.

Or for her to submit to mine.

Once we reach the guest room door, she stops, turning to face me. I do the same, the weight of my indecision bearing down on my shoulders. I should give Calista time away from me like she requested, but my need to be close to her, to reassure myself that she's safe, is a physical ache.

"Good night, Hayden."

I open my mouth to command her to walk to my room just as she opens the door to the guest room and steps inside. Now I'm the one who's hesitating. If my behavior didn't shock me, I might find my reluctance to take what I want amusing.

My palm slaps against the wood to prevent her from shutting the door. Calista blinks up at me in surprise, but her expression morphs into a frown when I stride up to her.

"What's wrong?" she asks, her voice tinged with suspicion.

"Considering what happened to you, I doubt I'll be able to sleep tonight. But I'll be damned if I'm alone in my bed. Not when the woman who embodies my deepest desires is under my roof."

She drops her gaze. Not before I catch the flicker of uncertainty in her eyes. "It's been a rough day..."

"You think I don't know that? Something inside me fucking died when I saw you lying there, covered in blood." I reach for Calista, taking her face between my hands and forcing her to look up at me. "I don't think you realize what that did to me, how it's *still* killing me."

Her eyes widen, surprise mixing with the vulnerability that she's been hiding from me. Now that I've seen it, I won't let it go. If there's a possibility that she wants me near, I'm going to pursue it until she can't deny it any longer.

For both our sakes.

And my sanity.

At this moment, we're suspended in time, the outside world ceasing to exist. The words between us, both spoken and silent, hang in the air like a breeze, thin and easy to dismiss. I suck in a deep breath as if to trap them before releasing them to Calista.

In the form of a kiss.

I tell her of my adoration, my loyalty, and my willingness to sacrifice anything for her. All without uttering a single word. It's a declaration that goes beyond sound, transcending the realm of spoken language.

She's quick to respond to my touch, shivering when I angle her head to deepen the kiss. The taste of her lips, the warmth of her skin against my hands, and the feel of her body flush with mine all collide inside me. They ignite a blaze of emotion that smolders deep within.

Both the dark *and* the light emotions.

Craving, sexual desire, and excitement are there, urging me to take Calista right here and now, to satiate my need for both her body and the woman herself. But these are the emotions that I've lived by for too long, the darkness that threatens to swallow me whole.

Awe, appreciation, and caring battle my other instincts with their light and purity, waging a war that could end with us healed—if I don't destroy them first.

My hunger for Calista, the starvation of both body and soul, rushes through me. I dominate her with my lips and my tongue while holding her prisoner to my desire. She moans softly and I'm quick to swallow the sound, the proof that I'm not alone in my desperation.

The kiss turns ravenous. I slide my fingers from her face to tangle them in her hair, anchoring her to me until the walls she erected tumble at my feet. Her response to me is fluid, a subtle shifting of her body as she melts into me, her thighs cradling my cock.

Calista doesn't realize she's offering the sweetest gift by yielding to me.

I rip my mouth from hers. She gazes up at me, her lips swollen and her eyes sparkling. I scrutinize her features, searching for any signs of regret or, worse, disgust.

"Calista," I rasp. Her name is an inquiry, a prayer, and a demand all in one.

"Hayden."

In the simple exchange of names and in the intensity of the emotions we share, I sense something profound. And real.

She rises on her toes to sweep her lips across mine in a

whisper of raw honesty, a reflection of the passion and acceptance she has for me. It might not be forgiveness, but it's more than I hoped for tonight.

I want Calista at a level that's deeper than physical intimacy. Something I refuse to name but know exists.

And how much I need it.

Our breaths merge in the space between us, and my pulse raps at an unsteady cadence, echoing with the significance of this moment. The openness in her eyes mirrors my own, creating a sense of unity and connection I've never experienced before.

I press my forehead to hers. "I need you."

"You have me."

"I won't be gentle."

She strokes my cheek with trembling fingers, her touch grounding me while exposing her trepidation. "I know."

CHAPTER 10

H ayden

I SLIDE MY HANDS DOWN HER SIDES, ENJOYING THE FEEL OF HER
enticing curves, and then grip her hips. When I grind my
cock against her with a groan, she wraps her arms around
my neck. Another show of surrender from her that has guilt
churning in my gut.

The things I want to do to her...

"I don't want to hurt you, Callie."

"I know," she says again, her tone stronger than before.

Is she trying to convince me or herself?

It doesn't matter. Once she whispered her understanding and acceptance of my intentions, any control I had
vanished.

I crush her mouth with mine, bruising her lips in my
urgency to taste her again. Despite her initial hesitance, she
returns the kiss with fervor. Satisfaction roars through me. I
walk her backward and deeper into the room until her legs

hit the edge of the bed. She falls back, pulling me down with her until the softness of her body is covered by the hardness of my own.

The kiss turns frantic as I roam my hands over her. I grip her breast before taking her nipple between my fingers, rolling it back and forth until she squirms beneath me.

"Don't hold back," I growl against her throat.

"What?"

I graze the sensitive part of her neck with my teeth, wringing a gasp from her. "You said that I have you, but I don't see it."

"I don't understand what you want."

I stare down at her, enjoying the sight of her plush lips and the way her hazel eyes shine with emotion. Her hair is splayed across the bed, the dark locks contrasting with the paleness of her skin. I want all of her because this woman has all of me.

"I want your heart, Callie."

"Hayden, I—"

"Don't tell me. Show me."

She uses her hold on my neck to pull me down for a kiss. It matches the intensity from before, but it's different because she's the one commanding me. I pour my need, along with my fear, into pleasuring her body, willing her to take everything I have to give. And the parts of me I'm reluctant to share.

Calista arches into me, her apprehension finally giving way to the passion between us without reservation. I revel in the moment until our clothes become a hindrance that I need to get rid of. Sitting back on my heels, I grip the hem of her shirt. She raises her arms out of obedience, and I remove the blouse, as well as her slacks.

I drag my fingers down her stomach, following the dip of

it until I reach her navel. She's a vision, a fantasy come to life, but imagining her pregnant makes my throat go dry. I want that almost as much as I want her to love me.

Good thing she went to the doctor I suggested, the one that I coerced into giving Calista a saline shot instead of the actual Depo. I'm going to put a baby in her. If not tonight, then soon...

Wearing only her bra and underwear now, Calista watches me as I shed my clothing. Her eyes grow wide when her gaze travels over my body. I take my cock in hand and stroke the length of it, smiling because she sucks in a breath.

"Tell me you want it," I say, continuing to slide my hand up and down.

"I want it."

"Try again."

She licks her lips. "I want you to fuck me, Hayden."

"First that mouth, and then that sweet cunt."

I crawl over her until the head of my cock rests against her chin. With one hand, I hold myself up while using the other to run my thumb across the seam of her lips. The caress is gentle, but I won't be.

"I can't tell you how long I've wanted to do this. Open for me." When she lets her jaw go slack, inviting me in, I shove my cock in her mouth with a loud groan. "Such a good fucking girl."

Her eyes widen in surprise before she seals her lips around me and begins to suck. Unable to stay still, I thrust in and out of her mouth, going deeper and deeper until my cock hits the back of her throat. Calista makes choking noises but doesn't stop the hard pulls of her mouth.

She squeezes her eyes shut as I move faster, the pleasure of fucking her mouth about to kill me. I grip her jaw gently to pry it open and withdraw my cock before I come on her tongue. Last time I gave her a "pearl necklace," but this time I want to give her a baby.

My baby.

She looks up at me, her lips still wet from sucking my cock. I groan and fist myself to keep from coming at the expression on her face. She's fucking gorgeous, but it's more than that. Her eyes are completely void of fear or nervousness. They're gleaming with anticipation.

Calista wants to get fucked.

As if in a trance, my hands move of their own accord, my fingers sliding down the side of her cheek before traveling along her slender neck. I could hurt her, ruin her, but she gazes up at me with trust. She might not have faith in me emotionally, but physically she has no issue surrendering to me.

I'm quick to remove her bra and underwear, ripping the fine lace from her body. She gasps at the violence simmering under my skin and in my touch but doesn't protest. I need her in a way I've never needed anyone before, and she must sense that.

Urgency presses along my psyche, pushing me to claim her. To mark her as mine. I lean down and press my lips to her breast, watching her grow flushed all over as I suck and nibble, leaving a trail of red blotches on her skin. She arches into my mouth, feeding my hunger while fanning its flames.

I'll never get enough of her.

I dig my fingers in her hips hard enough to leave bruises and yank her to me. She slides down the bed, her arms above her head. The sacrificial pose sets me off. My primal instincts roar to life, and I shove her thighs apart before driving into her.

Calista's tiny gasp barely penetrates my awareness. How

can it when I'm lost in her warmth and enveloped in her scent?

She tenses around me, her body trembling with every gyration of my hips. But I can't stop. When she relaxes underneath me and a moan brushes my ears, I know she's with me. I shift my hands to her waist to get a better grip on her and push her deeper into the mattress as I move faster, thrusting harder. Her head thrashes and her eyes flutter shut, but she takes it all.

My fingers biting into her skin.

The brutal thrusts.

It's pure fucking, carnal and wild.

Heat radiates from our bodies, both of us coated in a sheen of sweat that makes our skin slick. I can taste the salty flavor as I nip at her throat. She cries out, the sound a fusion of pleasure and pain. It excites me, throwing me over the edge.

Insanity takes over.

I withdraw from her, so quickly her cunt makes a suction noise. Then I'm flipping Calista onto her hands and knees before taking her from behind. The power of my thrusts has her hair swaying gently, the rhythmic movements increasing in speed as I push my body to its limit.

She groans, the low sound muffled in the bedding, but I hear it. Relish it. However, the sight of the gauze taped to her shoulder nearly breaks my concentration. It's a painful reminder of reality, of the danger that lurks nearby. My emotions heighten, becoming riotous and volatile, until I gather them with the intent to channel them into Calista.

I control her pleasure, and tonight is no different. I take command over every sensation, bending her will to mine with the intent to give her everything she desires. Her body responds, her cunt tightening around my cock every time I drive deeper, my mind spinning from the knowledge she belongs to me.

Her moans grow louder and louder until I reach around to stroke her clit, forcing a scream from her throat. She's exquisite when she comes. Her orgasm triggers my own, my spine tingling before I'm undone.

This is my moment of surrender...to the woman who's completely unaware.

I collapse on top of her, my cheek resting on her back, my arms shaking with the effort it takes to hold my weight. Calista remains silent, her body rising and falling with each jagged breath. I close my eyes as both exhaustion and contentment settle on me. My connection to her is so strong that I'm reluctant to tear myself away.

Especially since I'm unsure if she hates me for using her body selfishly.

CHAPTER 11

H ayden

CALISTA SIGHS. THE SWEET SOUND GRAZES MY EARS BEFORE gripping my soul. How can she rest so peacefully after I just fucked the shit out of her?

I needed her with an intensity that overwhelmed me. It broke my self-control and sent me spiraling into a dark place where my only thought was to claim her. But it wasn't just that. I was desperate to reassure myself she was alive and mine to keep.

What I did to her was brutal. Violent. I might've warned her that I wouldn't be gentle, but that couldn't have prepared Calista for how hard and fast I took her. Almost as though I was punishing her for getting hurt. It wasn't her fault by any means. The fear of losing Calista choked the life out of me until I couldn't breathe unless I was inside her, feeling her body all around mine.

My desperation for her has never been this strong.

And it's continuing to grow.

I ease from her body with my teeth clenched, battling the urge to slam back into her. My cock, semi-hard, readies itself at the idea. Ignoring that greedy fucker, I shift Calista and take up a position next to her, lying on my side with her pressed against me.

I run my gaze over her, taking in the light sprinkle of bruises that are already beginning to bloom on her skin. They're not only from my hands, but my teeth and mouth, and anything else I could touch her with. Brand her with. The marks covering her breasts, hips, neck, and shoulders will remind her tomorrow what transpired between us tonight.

What we shared wasn't only passion. It was something deeper. She met my fire with her own, matching me in ferocity while maintaining her sweet disposition. By offering her body, she soothed the demons inside of me, replacing them with a peace I never thought was possible. Even now, I'm calm, despite her injury staring me in the face. Though whenever I look at the gauze covering her wound, my stomach clenches.

I brush back a stray lock of hair that's plastered to her damp cheek. Calista's tears have yet to dry. Did she cry from pain or pleasure? Maybe both.

"Callie?"

"Hmm?"

I nearly laugh at the disgruntled sound. My smile is bright in the darkness. "Are you all right?"

"Define 'all right.'"

With a firm but gentle hand, I shift Calista onto her back so I can see her face. "Did I hurt you?"

She gives me an exasperated look that amuses me more than anything. "Define 'hurt.'" When I narrow my gaze in warning, she blows out a breath. "Yes, you hurt me."

"I figured as much." I trail my fingers over the red star-bursts on her breasts. "I want to say I'm sorry, but it'd be a lie. I enjoy seeing you this way, with the evidence of me fucking you all over your skin."

My cock stirs in response to looking at her. As it always does. I bring my gaze back to her face, trying to focus on something other than taking her again.

"I'm talking about you hurting my feelings, Hayden, not my body. I'm not sore because the pain medication is still in my system."

"I see."

"Do you really? I doubt it. Not that I'd ever lie to you, but if I did, there's no way you'd be okay with it."

I dip my head in agreement. "The severity of my actions would depend on what you hid from me."

"And if I invaded your privacy by stalking you?"

"I'd be flattered."

She glares at me. "Be serious."

"I am. You're all I've ever wanted, so I'd enjoy having you pursue me that way. It shows enthusiasm, dedication, and focus."

"You're insane," she mutters.

"I am crazy about you, Callie. I never said otherwise."

"What am I going to do with you?" Her voice is just below a whisper, a tiny breath skimming my mouth.

"Stay with me. Love me."

She blinks up at me, the surprise in her eyes sure to be found in mine. Just because I told her the truth doesn't mean I had any intention of revealing it. At least not right now, when she's still uncertain about me in general.

I want her to love me for selfish reasons that she wouldn't understand.

"What did you say?" she asks.

"You heard me."

"Well, I want to hear it again." When I give her a pointed look, she reaches up to clasp my face between her hands. "Please."

I growl low in my throat. "You know how I feel about you begging me."

"Why do you think I'm doing it?"

"Is it really that important to you?"

When she nods, I roll it over in my mind. In my profession, if there's ever an opportunity to use something to further my negotiations, I won't hesitate to use it. Especially with the woman underneath me. She holds all of the power.

"I want you to love me, Callie."

"What about *you* loving *me*?"

When I remain silent, her words repeating themselves in my brain, she drops her hands. "That's what I thought. You want me to give you everything, but you refuse to share yourself with me. I've never met someone who's such a hypocrite."

I grit my teeth, already missing the feel of her touch on my skin. "I don't know if it's possible for me to love anyone."

"Yes, it is. You love yourself. That's why you act the way you do. The lying and hidden agendas all lead you to getting what you want. It doesn't matter what my needs are or how you hurt me in the process."

"I don't think I can give you what you want."

"Why?" Her eyes glisten with tears, born of anger and pain. "What are you afraid of?"

I shift on the bed, lying beside her to stare up at the ceiling. Her question is valid. I'm man enough to admit that. But my answer isn't as easy to recognize. Not like the fear.

The only thing in this world that scares me is the thought of losing Calista.

"Being vulnerable," I say. "I never want to feel weak."

She rolls onto her side, her stare centered on my profile. "Love doesn't make you weak. It gives you the strength to fight for something worth having. Love should bring joy and fulfillment, not sadness and emptiness."

My lips twist with disbelief. "It might be the most painful emotion in existence."

"Only if you're not with the person you love."

"That's exactly my point."

Calista goes quiet. After a few moments, she crawls on top of me, settling her hips on mine and her hands on my chest. The silky tendrils of her hair graze my arms, and the softness of her skin brushes mine, but it's her eyes that hold me prisoner. The hazel swirls with compassion, to an extent I've never seen from her before.

If that's not love, it's pretty damn close...

"In your own twisted way, you love me, Hayden."

She lifts a brow in challenge, waiting for me to respond. I can only look at her and wait for a denial to come barreling to the forefront of my mind. It does, but not because I don't care for her.

I can't risk loving her.

"Calista..."

"Say it." She digs her nails into my skin, her gaze just as piercing. "Say you don't love me."

I match her glare. "You don't really want to hear that."

She leans down until her breasts are flush with my chest and her lips hover above mine. "Yes, I do. I need to know here and now if you're able to tell me the truth when it

70

matters most. Because if you lie to me about this, I swear to God, Hayden, I'll leave you."

"The fuck you will." My jaw tightens as I grab her hips, digging my fingers into her soft flesh. "How will you know I'm lying?"

"A woman's intuition."

She holds my gaze. And then moves her hips, sliding her wet pussy along the length of my cock.

"Don't start shit you can't finish," I say, my voice gruff. "If you don't stop, you will get fucked."

"Maybe."

Her movements are slow and deliberate, as if she's daring me to stop her. When my cum begins to leak from her and onto my stomach, I reach out to swipe it with my fingers. Then I shove two of them back inside her.

"What are you doing?" she asks on a groan.

"Putting my cum where it belongs."

She shakes her head. "No, you're trying to distract me."

"Are you serious? You're the one rubbing your pretty pussy all over my dick, and you think I'm a distraction?"

I stroke her until she's riding my hand, grinding down on it while glaring at me. "Fuck, Hayden."

For once, I don't scold her for her language. Instead, I reward that dirty mouth by curling my fingers, focusing on the spot that'll give her what she wants.

"Please." Calista bows her head as though praying. Maybe she is. Right now, I'm her god. "Please tell me."

I wait until her breath hitches, until her lips part on a silent scream. The moment she comes, when she's the most vulnerable to her body's needs. And me. I whisper the words then, my truth, whether or not she can accept it.

"I don't want to love you."

But I do.

CHAPTER 12

C alista

Warm sunlight filters through the curtains, rousing me from a deep and peaceful sleep. For a moment, I'm disoriented, still caught in the hazy remnants of a dream. Then it all comes flooding back.

Hayden fucking me like a savage.

His words to me.

My submission to him.

I stretch languidly, the soreness in my muscles a delicious reminder of last night. With a frown I roll over, silently wondering why Hayden isn't holding me, but discover his side of the bed is empty. I reach out to find his spot cool to the touch. He must have woken up early.

As I sit up, the sheet slips down to pool around my naked waist. I take a moment to admire the love bites blooming across my breasts and hips, vivid souvenirs of his claiming. Heat pools low in my belly at the memories they invoke.

After his raw, emotional confession last night, our ensuing intimacy had felt different...more tender and connected. With each reverent caress and kiss, I felt the ice around Hayden's heart melting.

When he finally joined our bodies for the second time, there was a new sensitivity to his touch, as if I were something infinitely precious. And later, wrapped in each other's arms and spent, he whispered, "Please, don't make me love you."

My breath still catches remembering those words. It's the closest thing to a declaration of love I've gotten from him. Part of me remains wary, afraid to hope after so much heartbreak. But a larger part now feels certain he cares for me just as deeply as I care for him.

Maybe he said doesn't want to love me because he already does...

I slide from the bed and rummage through Hayden's drawer, searching for one of his t-shirts to wear. After putting on a soft gray one that stops mid-thigh on me, I inhale the scent of him underneath the smell of detergent. This man makes my pulse race without even trying.

Standing in the middle of his room, I stare at the black-and-white picture above his dresser. Even though the woman's face is away from the viewer, she's beautiful. Her profile is dainty, and her body is well-proportioned, but that's not what makes her attractive. It's the air of mystery that surrounds her, as though she's on her way to meet her lover for the last time.

Looking at this photograph stirs up the insecurity I felt the first time I was in Hayden's bedroom. Add that to the shyness I'm experiencing this morning, and I'm tempted to dive back under the covers.

The scent of coffee invades my senses, a reminder that the man encompassing my thoughts is waiting for me. I leave the bedroom and walk down the hallway, stopping to pause just outside the kitchen. Hayden stands with his back to me. His hair is messy and sticking up in some areas, but that only makes him more attractive. Well, that and his bare chest and the sweatpants hanging low on his hips.

I stare in shock. It never crossed my mind that someone like Hayden, a man who's always dressed to impress, would own sweatpants, let alone wear them.

My heart beats faster the longer I look at him. I want to greet him and let him know I'm standing there, but my mouth is dry, and I can't form words. I'm not shy anymore. I've been struck stupid.

He turns to face me and leans against the island, the muscles in his torso flexing. "Good morning, Callie."

"Hi." It comes out as a squeak, and my cheeks heat with embarrassment. This man has fucked me ten ways from Sunday, and I can't greet him without being self-conscious? Unbelievable.

"Come here," he says. When I remain still, he frowns. "What's wrong? Is your injury bothering you?"

"No, I mean, yes. Wait. I need a second." I take a deep breath and release it slowly. It does nothing to rid me of my nerves, and I give up trying. "Who's the woman in the picture hanging on your bedroom wall?"

"Come here, and I'll answer you."

I lift my chin. "Answer me, and I'll come to you."

"Oh, you'll *come* all right."

He stalks toward me. A tiny shriek leaves me—half excitement, half surprise—but I stand my ground with my heart thrashing in my chest. When he's only inches away, I throw up my hands, palms facing him.

"My stitches feel tight," I say. "Please don't grab me."

Hayden comes to an abrupt halt. He towers over me, staring down at me with concern etched into his features. "Instead of interrogating me about a photograph, you should've mentioned your discomfort."

I shrug, and immediately regret it when the movement pulls the skin of my shoulder taut. "Well, I'm telling you now."

"I'll get your medication."

"I just hate how sleepy I get when I take it."

He does an about-face to head back into the kitchen. I sag against the wall, careful not to lean on my wound, taking a moment to catch my breath. There's no doubt in my mind that Hayden would've fucked me right then if I hadn't spoken up about my stitches paining me.

His appetite is insatiable. Although I'm not complaining, I wonder how much his need for dominance motivates it. He uses sex as a power tactic, but would he keep doing it if I gave in?

When he returns with a glass of water and pills in hand, he offers them to me. I'm quick to down the medication. "The woman in the black-and-white picture. Who is she, Hayden?"

The side of his mouth lifts. "Why is this so important to you?"

"You better not laugh at me. This is serious."

"I'm not going to tease you about this. You can stop looking at me like you want to strangle me." He tilts his head. "Are you jealous, Callie?"

Yes.

I scoff. "Don't let my question inflate your already large

ego. Who is she, and why is she on your bedroom wall, of all places?"

He leans down until I can see the blue of his eyes sparkling with amusement and pleasure. "It's you."

"*Me*?"

"Yes."

I spin on my heel and race to the bedroom, Hayden's laughter following me. The sound, carefree and joyous, has my heart squeezing in on itself. This is only the third time I've heard him laugh. I might like the dark and broody part of his personality, but this is something special.

After coming to a hard stop in front of the dresser, I stare up at the photo. I barely notice Hayden coming to stand behind me until he leans forward to place his mouth next to my ear.

"The only woman I'll allow in this room is you."

"I can't believe it," I whisper. "God, you are such a stalker."

He laughs again, and I press my lips together to fight back a smile. I haven't exactly forgiven him for that stunt, but after dealing with the nightmare from my past, Hayden is the only person that makes me feel safe. Ironic, since he scared the shit out of me in the beginning.

"I plead guilty," he says. He drags his lips down the side of my neck, placing an open-mouthed kiss on the sensitive skin there. I shiver, evidence that my body obeys him more than it does me. "I took this picture to keep from kidnapping you."

"Am I supposed to give you an award for that?" I huff. "How long ago was this?"

"The week after your father's funeral."

I stiffen. "Are you saying you've been following me for months?"

Hayden grabs my shoulders, careful to avoid my injury, and turns me to face him. "I needed to know what kind of woman you were. Now that I know, I'm never going back to life without you. I can't."

"I don't know if I can, either."

He tightens his hold on me. "I want to kiss you so badly."

"Why don't you?"

"Because if I do, I'll fuck you, and I have to leave soon."

"Let me guess, I have to stay here all day?" When he nods, I roll my eyes. "I know this may come as a shock to you, but I like working and staying busy."

Instead of arguing with me, he presses a kiss to my forehead. The tender action leaves me staring up at him in shock. First Hayden's laughing, and now he's being sweet... How can I not forgive him? Maybe I already have, or I wouldn't have given him every part of me last night.

"Callie, I know you don't want to hear this, but someone sent you that package to frighten you. Until I know who they are and what they want from you, I'm going to do everything in my power to keep you safe."

I place my hands on his chest. "Do you think I'm in danger?"

"I'm not willing to take a chance with your life."

"That's not an answer."

He averts his gaze in a rare show of uncertainty. Or maybe it's to hide his fear..."Someone killed your father and his lover and assaulted his daughter. I think this mysterious person has a vendetta against the senator. With him being deceased, you're the only target left. Let's not dismiss the fact that both you and his secretary had the same drug compound in your systems on the night the crimes took place. It's all too connected to be coincidental."

I slowly nod my head, absorbing this information. It's

nothing new, but hearing it all at once after everything that happened yesterday puts it into perspective. Someone has to solve this case and bring the person behind it to justice, or I'll always have to look over my shoulder, waiting for someone to come after me.

"Why now?" I ask. "My father's funeral was months ago. If this person thought to hurt me, then why didn't they do it when I first moved out of my father's estate?"

"Maybe because they saw someone stalking you and it kept them at a distance?"

When Hayden winks at me, I nearly melt into the floor. His expression turns serious, and he blows out a breath. "All jokes aside, I don't have an answer for you. What I do know is that I'll get to the bottom of this. Until I do, I'm going to need you to make good on the promise you made me."

I scrunch my head in confusion. "Which one? You demand a lot of things."

"You promised to let me protect you."

"Oh, right. At least this prison is comfortable."

"You're not staying here."

CHAPTER 13

C alista

"WHAT?" I SQUINT UP AT HIM. "WHERE ARE YOU SENDING me?"

He slides his hands from my shoulders to encircle my neck and pulls me toward him. Despite the gentleness of his touch, his eyes are hard with determination. "*We* are leaving. I don't want you in the city while I work on this case. Pack your bags for somewhere warm."

I hold his intense stare, refusing to back down. If I give in on this, who knows what other freedoms he'll strip from me under the excuse of protecting me?

"I can't just leave," I say. "I have a job, and I'll miss Harper. Besides, what about your promise to me? I want to enroll for classes in the spring, which is only a few weeks away. I understand you wanting to keep me safe, and I believe you'll do that, but it'll have to be here. If you trust me, then you have to back off and let me make my own choices."

His expression remains stony despite my impassioned plea. I search his eyes for a sign he'll bend on this, but there's no softness to be found. If anything, he's more rigid than before.

"I understand you wanting your independence," he says between clenched teeth. "But I won't risk your life just so you can enjoy the familiar comforts of home. I've made too many mistakes where you're concerned, and I won't add another to the list."

"Do you mean the mistake of leaving those pearls in your pocket?" I jerk from his hold with a laugh, but the sound is hollow. "That was a huge mistake. It showed me I can't trust you not to put your needs above mine."

He works his jaw, visibly struggling with inner turmoil before narrowing his eyes. "I'm not changing my mind, Calista. Pack your bags or don't. Either way, we're leaving."

My heart sinks. "I don't get a say in this?" I ask, bitterness coating my words. "You just get to decide what's best for my life, and that's it, end of discussion?"

"It's for your own good." He folds his arms, a silent indication that the subject is closed.

I rear back as though he slapped me. Indignation and hurt well up inside my chest, nearly bursting through my skin. "I won't accept that. You can't dictate every aspect of my life and dress it up as protection."

"Say what you want, but you're not leaving this place until I come back for you. When I do, you're getting on the plane, even if I have to carry you. Whether you're tied up or not, that's your choice."

I give him a saccharine smile. "How kind of you to let me

have a say. What about my body? Will you take that whenever you feel like it, too?"

Hayden's eyes flash at the implication right before he steps toward me. I retreat, but he keeps advancing until my back hits a flat surface. He slams his palms against the wall on either side of my head, caging me in. It doesn't matter. I don't have the strength to run, not with the look of fury covering his face and draining me of my courage.

"I would never force myself on you," he grinds out. "I'm not a rapist. Don't insult me or what we have by suggesting it. However..."

He presses the length of his body to mine, pinning me in place. I gasp at the feel of his cock, hard and pulsing against me. My cheeks burn from both arousal and shame. I crossed a line, but I can't take it back, even if I regret what I said because of anger.

"Miss Green, if you think that I won't seduce you until you're begging me to fuck you, then think again. I don't have a problem playing with that pretty pussy until you're crying to come."

"Miss Green? I thought it was Mrs. Bennett, according to Sebastian," I snap, my words sharp and my breaths thin.

"Mrs. Bennett has a nice ring to it. It'd look even better written on your skin."

I glare at Hayden, knowing I failed to get a reaction from him. "What we have is a joke, *Mr. Bennett*. You only want me if you can control every aspect of our relationship."

"Sounds like marriage to me."

"You arrogant son of a bitch."

"Call me what you want," Hayden says, "but remember that name because it'll be the one you're screaming later, *Mrs. Bennett*."

He shoves away from the wall, his jaw set in a hard line.

Without speaking another word, he turns away from me and strides into the bathroom, slamming the door behind him. I stand there clutching my chest, willing my heart to calm and my panicked breaths to even out.

Seeing Hayden this angry with me...I never want to experience it again.

I stumble from his room to the guest bedroom and sink onto the edge of the mattress. Time passes while I stare ahead, still in shock from the confrontation. The distance between us feels insurmountable, and from the looks of things, we'll never come to a peaceful agreement.

Unless I surrender.

I GRAB MY PHONE FROM THE NIGHTSTAND IN HAYDEN'S ROOM without wincing. Relief due to the pain medication is in full effect, but the pain from my conversation with Hayden earlier still lingers. He hasn't contacted me since he left for work. I'm grateful, but lonely.

On the screen of my cell phone is a notification from Harper. I smile, despite my battered emotions, and open up the text.

> Harper: Hey girl, I know you're busy resting, but when you get a moment, send me a text. I'm trying not to freak out. Okay, that's a lie. I'm totally freaked the fuck out over you. Message me when you get this.

> Harper: I don't know if the pain meds they gave you are working, but if not, let me know. My mom works for some big-name pharmaceutical company, and I can get you the good shit.

Calista: Hi friend. I'm sorry I made you worry. After I saw you in the hospital, I was discharged. Then Hayden drove me to the pharmacy to pick up my medication, and we went back to his place to eat dinner. After that, I passed out. How's Alex? Can you tell him that I'm sorry and I'll pay for all of the damages once I get back to work?

Harper responds within seconds. I smile as I picture her typing furiously on her cell phone while ignoring everyone around her. Once she has her sights set on something, good luck getting her attention.

Harper: It's about time you messaged me. I was thiiiis close to breaking into the penthouse, or whatever fancy-as-fuck place you live. Yesterday, Alex and I cleaned up all of the glass, tossed all of the baked goods to ensure they didn't hurt anyone, and then spent the rest of the day baking in the kitchen. Don't worry about trying to compensate Alex for anything. Your husband—I believe I heard that Russian god refer to you as Mrs. Bennett—arranged for someone to arrive today and fix everything. He paid for all of it too, and he gave Alex the amount of revenue he would've made if we'd been open.

Calista: Wow.

Harper: Yup. When it comes to you, that attorney does not fuck around.

Calista: You're telling me.

Harper: I am telling you. You should've seen his face when he came to the Sugar Cube and saw you lying on the floor. I'm not religious, but I said three Hail Marys. That man looked like he wanted to kill someone, and it wasn't going to be me. Anyway, when are you coming back to work? I'll be opening tomorrow. Fuck my life.

I gnaw on my bottom lip, thinking about the travel plans Hayden mentioned this morning. As much as I want to rebel, I'm not sure I want to provoke him again. But if I don't, then what?

Calista: I'm not sure. Hayden said he wants to take me on an impromptu vacation while he figures out who sent me that delivery.

Harper: You know, maybe getting away from all of this bullshit wouldn't be such a bad idea. Alex finally hired two more people, and Sheryl is back from maternity leave. For once, we won't be short-staffed. So, if you're worried about that, don't be.

Calista: You know me so well. I'll try not to feel guilty about all of this.

Harper: You better not. None of this is your fault. I've got to run. Some asshole is trying to talk to me and I'm about to tell my economics professor he can take his syllabus and jack off with it. Talk about micro, am I right? ;)

Calista: lol. Ttyl. <3

I flop onto the bed and stare up at the ceiling in a daze. Harper made Hayden's suggestion to leave the city sound reasonable. But whenever I think about the way he ordered me to pack my things, I want to hit something. If I don't stand up to him now, will I regret it later?

A sigh escapes me, filling the quiet. I don't have any answers, only questions. Not all of them center around Hayden. Who took my panties and sent them to me almost a year after my assault? I shudder at the thought of someone holding on to them for this long. That's sick.

What do they want from me? I don't have anything of value. My family name is in tatters. I don't have even a fraction of the wealth I used to. I don't own anything expensive, whether that be something physical or by way of secret or privileged information. Nothing makes sense.

My anger toward Hayden lessens enough for my muscles to relax and loosen a little. He's an asshole, but that man wants to get rid of the danger looming over me. How can I make him value my independence while staying in the shadow of his protection?

CHAPTER 14

C alista

THE LAST STREAKS OF SUNLIGHT FILTER INTO THE ROOM, giving it a bronzed glow. One of the rays creeps along my face, warming it slightly and penetrating the darkness of sleep. I scrunch up my face with a yawn and my eyes flutter open, fighting the tendrils of lethargy still clinging to me.

They vanish the second I sense that I'm not alone.

I sit straight up and wait for my stitches to pain me from the swift movement. I immediately forget about my injury the second a pair of light blue eyes meet mine. Even in the dimly lit room, I can make out the concern shining in their depths.

"Hayden," I breathe. My body tenses, waiting for him to touch me.

He nods, but remains standing at the foot of the bed with his arms folded. This man has never had a problem expressing what he wants. I brush a strand of hair away from my cheek and wait.

"I take it you rested today?" he asks.

"Yes."

"Good. Did you pack your things? We're leaving before dawn."

I hold his stare, my insides quivering. "No."

"I see." His mild tone is at odds with the thinning of his mouth. "You've made your choice, then."

"Why are you doing this? Forcing me to go with you is kidnapping, just so you know. I'm pretty sure there are laws forbidding this type of thing."

He quirks a brow. "You must be feeling better if you're bold enough to lecture me on the workings of the law. I can narrate this situation in a way that doesn't make anything I'm doing illegal, but there's no point. You're coming with me because whoever sent you that package has an agenda."

I shake my head in denial. "How can you be so sure someone wants to hurt me?"

"Who can predict or understand the mind of a deranged person?"

I give him a pointed look.

"Be careful, Mrs. Bennett."

"You really think it has something to do with my father?" I ask, attempting to change the subject. And pointedly ignoring his new name for me.

Hayden nods. "Politicians rarely take and maintain an office without some type of dirt on them."

"My father was a good man. If you care about me at all, you won't say negative things about him in front of me." I drop my gaze and smooth out the comforter, unable to look at Hayden. "I want my memories of him to remain intact, regardless of what your investigation turns up."

"I understand." His voice softens, giving me the courage to meet his gaze. "Your father was innocent of the charges brought against him. I know this now, but I should've known he was a decent man after meeting you. If that wasn't true, he would've killed the goodness in you instead of nurturing it."

"Thank you. It means a lot to me to hear you say something nice about my father. God, I miss him so much."

Hayden stiffens. It's nearly imperceptible, but I catch it regardless. Narrowing my gaze, I scrutinize him, searching his face for any detail that could explain his change in demeanor.

"I owe you an apology concerning your father," he says quietly. "I severely misjudged him."

"It's okay. You've admitted that you changed your opinion of him, and that's all that matters to me."

He shoves his hands in his pockets and turns his head toward the sliver of waning sunlight now failing to illuminate the room. "I was so wrong, and I can never make it up to you."

My forehead scrunches in confusion. Just as I'm about to ask him to explain what he's talking about, Hayden faces me, his expression stoic once more. The abrupt change in him leaves me speechless. Something's clearly bothering him, but I have no idea what it could be.

Or if I want to know.

"I'm assuming you haven't eaten dinner since you were asleep when I walked in here," he says.

"I haven't. When did you get home?"

He lifts a shoulder in a half-shrug. "Hours ago."

"You didn't watch me the whole time, did you?"

"Yes, I did." He pauses and then says, "Seeing you asleep

in my bed puts me at ease. I'm still fucking terrified at the thought of losing you."

My heart pounds wildly in my chest at his confession. This isn't the first time Hayden's admitted to being scared of losing me, but for some reason this is different. It's filled with more than fear.

There's pure agony etched into every word, every syllable.

An eerie silence descends on the room, blanketing us in tension. I break it with a whisper, barely discernible to my own ears. "I don't know what to say, Hayden."

He breaks eye contact with me, his jaw tightening as he looks away. "Unless you're agreeing to cooperate, there's nothing to be said."

"That's not true. Despite my past coming back to haunt me, you and I have issues that need to be resolved. If not..." Now I'm the one who's turning my head when his gaze snaps in my direction. "Things need to change."

"They will once this threat is neutralized."

I exhale my pent-up frustration. "Yeah, okay."

"Maybe once you've eaten, your sour disposition will improve."

"Unless you've decided you're not going to kidnap me, then I doubt it," I mutter.

Hayden extends his hand to assist me. "I have rope set aside, should you require it."

I shove his hand away and slide from the mattress. Before my feet have a chance to fully land on the soft rug, he snakes an arm around my waist and hauls me to him. I slam against his chest in a daze.

"Rejection only makes me want you more," he says. "Keep fighting me, and I'll be fucking you on the dining table."

Hearing the passion in his voice has my body reacting, despite my best efforts. His sensual threat, combined with the intensity of our exchange, stirs something within me I can't ignore. It's an emotional connection that we've forged, one that transcends the circumstances we're struggling to navigate.

I inhale deeply in an attempt to steady my breathing. With him holding me this close, it's impossible. "I'm hungry," I say, my voice trembling as I fight my need for him.

He releases me, but doesn't step back. Once again, he offers his hand. This time, I take it without hesitation. Provoking him again will instigate a battle I can't win.

Side by side, we make our way to the kitchen. Thoughts zip through my mind, pinging different worries and insecurities until I'm ready to get drunk to avoid thinking at all. Whenever I run through the possible scenarios concerning this getaway he's planned, I can't come up with anything that'd make peace between us.

"What's the destination for tomorrow?"

Hayden lifts my hand and grazes the inside of my wrist with his lips before answering. "A tropical island far from here."

I tug on his hold, unable to concentrate while he's kissing my skin. He releases me with a knowing smile, and I resist the urge to make a face at him.

"Could you be any vaguer?" I ask.

"The less you know, the better. The same goes for your friend. "

"Fine."

Telling Harper wouldn't do me any good. It's not as if she's going to rescue me from him. Then there's the possibility that Hayden's lying to protect me, per his usual.

"What do you want to eat?" he asks, interrupting my musings.

"It doesn't matter. Your housekeeper is such a good cook. I haven't tasted anything that I haven't loved. I'd like to meet her at some point."

"In time."

He walks over to the stainless-steel refrigerator and removes two covered plates. After heating the contents, he sets them on the dining table, one right across from the other.

I take a seat with my mouth watering, ready to devour the entire portion of lasagna. Hayden settles in the other chair. He watches me, unmoving.

A blush rises to my cheeks. I duck my head and reach for my utensils, using my food as a focal point. Even though I'm not looking at him, I can feel his gaze following every one of my movements. I wait for him to eat, but his plate remains untouched, his attention never leaving me.

I shift under his watchful stare, silently reprimanding myself for letting him get to me. "You're staring."

"I know."

I snap my head up. He meets my wide gaze with a soft expression, one that's rarely shown. It's almost reverent, as if I'm the most captivating thing he's ever seen. The intense energy flowing off of him sends a thrill through me. I immediately suppress it.

"You're so beautiful, Calista."

Bowing my head once more, I ignore my flustered state and take another bite, savoring the rich flavors. "Can we bring your housekeeper to wherever the fuck you're taking me?"

Hayden coughs to hide his amusement. "Language, Mrs. Bennett. And no, we won't take Cecil with us."

"Well, I tried."

"You do realize that I don't want to deny you anything, right?"

I shrug.

"And you know I'd do anything to keep you safe, right?"

"Yes, that's what worries me," I say with a nod. "You don't have healthy boundaries."

He tilts his head. "Are you saying love should have boundaries?"

"Are you saying you love me?"

"I think it's inevitable."

My heart quickens at that, but I roll my eyes to mask it. "You're such a romantic."

"Do you love me, Calista?"

I stop breathing until my lungs cry out for relief. During those seconds, Hayden watches me with a hungry expression, as if he's starving for my affection.

"Right now, I don't even like you. Stalker, kidnapper, dictator, etc. Should I continue?"

"Details." He waves a hand in dismissal. "Answer the question."

"Why does it matter to you?"

"Because I've never met anyone like you." He leans forward, his gaze unwavering. "Calista, you challenge me, intrigue me, but you're the only person to make me question everything I've ever known."

"And you think that's love?"

He reclines back in his chair with a thoughtful expression. "I think it's profound. You're irreplaceable. I'd be an idiot to think I could have this with another woman, when I've never wanted anything more than a quick fuck. Until you."

I chew on my lower lip as a tiny bit of hope swirls within me. "You're impossible, you know that?"

He gives me a sad smile that pricks at my heart. "I've been told that once or twice in my life."

"By whom?"

"My mother."

The simple answer carries a depth and weight that I can't leave alone. It's a reminder that beneath the hardened exterior of this man, Hayden is a person with his own history, pain, and complexities.

"I'm sorry I brought it up," I say quietly.

"It's fine. Although I think about her constantly, I've never spoken about her until now."

"What changed?"

"You."

"Don't try to flatter me," I say. "For once, tell me the truth."

All traces of amusement leave his face. "You're the first person that I ever wanted to share her memory with."

"Oh."

He doesn't wait for me to gather my thoughts and shape them into a coherent sentence. After getting to his feet, he extends his hand. "Come on, it's time for bed."

"What if I'm not tired?"

"You will be."

With a lifted chin, I rest my hand in his and get to my feet. "You're right. The walk to the guest bedroom is really long."

"Your sarcasm isn't necessary," he says, his lips twitching.

"Neither is your arrogance, but here we are."

He shakes his head with a sigh. "Come on, let's get you to bed."

I stop my feet, but my heart continues racing with nerves and curiosity. "Wait."

"What is it?"

I take a fortifying breath before continuing. "If I admitted to loving you, what would you do?"

He slowly turns to face me. His eyes hold mine, a flicker of surprise lighting up their depths. The silence grows, charged with both anticipation and dread. Within seconds, I'm full of regret.

"Never m—"

"Calista, I don't know what I'd do because I've never been in love. But if you were to admit your feelings for me, I would cherish and protect them until I die."

"That's very similar to a marriage vow."

He gives me a secret smile. "Give it time."

CHAPTER 15

C alista

I'M NOT SURE IF IT'S THE PAIN MEDS OR THE EMOTIONALLY charged day I had, but I'm ready to pass out. If this is how my body reacts to regular medication, I can't imagine what the "good shit" would be like. It makes me wonder if Harper has personal experience with certain prescription drugs because of her mother's job.

Inside the bathroom, I quickly undress, frowning when I see a bandage on my hip. I might be groggy from my medication, but not to the point that I've forgotten having another injury. Trepidation courses through me as I peel away the medical tape with trembling fingers. The first glimpse of the black ink has me gasping, but I nearly scream when I yank it back completely.

Mrs. Bennett.

The tattoo is a beautiful script, one that I would've picked if given the choice. Only I wasn't.

My breaths come out in angry puffs until I'm ready to explode. I lose track of time as I stand there, debating how to handle this, but all I can think is: *Fucking Hayden*.

When the room is full of steam and I'm beginning to sweat, I sigh in defeat. There's nothing I can do about the tattoo right now. What I *can* do is not give Hayden the satisfaction of knowing it bothers me.

I replace the bandage and step into the shower. The hot water does nothing to ease the tension in my body. Once I'm finished, I wrap a towel around my torso, constantly glancing at the door. Even though Hayden didn't disturb me, I'm still anticipating his presence in the bathroom. Having a quiet moment wasn't actually peaceful, but when it comes to him, nothing is.

Except the times I trusted him completely.

I release a wistful sigh. Before I knew he was my stalker, I was tumbling head over heels in love with him. Even now, I'm probably a lost cause, but something inside me is holding on to my independence. He's trying just as hard to strip me of it. One of us is going to give in and I highly suspect it's me.

How does someone fight a hurricane without being swept away and drowned?

I shake my head at my thoughts and quickly throw on underwear and a bra, along with a pair of shorts and a matching floral top. The thin straps leave my injury free of chafing, which is one of the reasons I chose it. The other is to avoid giving Hayden the wrong idea by wearing a silky teddy. He can't keep his hands off of me as it is.

With a frown, I recall my inability to say no to him. Every time he's initiated sex with a demanding kiss or a light caress, my fortitude melts like a snowflake in the palm of my hand.

"Callie?"

"I'll be right out."

After turning the doorknob, I step into Hayden's bedroom and near darkness. The only light comes from the moon's rays, casting the man of my dreams and nightmares in shadow. He stands by the window, wearing nothing except a pair of pants meant for sleep.

I jerk my gaze from his ripped stomach and the lines that disappear inside the waistband sitting low on his hips. Nervousness travels along my arms like crackles of electricity, and I nearly jump when Hayden motions me to him. With a small shake of my head, I plant my feet.

"We need to talk about something."

He lifts a brow. "We've done nothing except talk all evening."

"I know, but this is important to me."

There's a subtle shift in his body, a softening that wasn't there before. "I'm listening."

"I need a time-out on the sex."

The change in Hayden is immediate. His eyes narrow to little more than slits, and his entire frame goes rigid with suppressed ire. "What is this? A fucking game of tag?"

"No, it's not." I wrap my arms around my middle to fortify myself against the anger he's exuding in waves. "There's so much going on in my life right now, beginning with you admitting to being my stalker and ending with someone who's decided to take that title by sending me those panties. I'm worried that I won't be able to make logical decisions as long as we're intimate, and it clouds my emotions."

He tilts his head, his expression full of disbelief. I bite the inside of my cheek to keep from talking and saying anything else that'll piss him off more.

"What decision is there to make?" he asks, his voice deceptively quiet.

"Whether I can forgive you for lying to me, with the knowledge that you'll continue to do so."

"You will forgive me. It's just a matter of when."

I glare at him, some of the anxiousness seeping from me to be replaced with anger. "How do you know?"

"Because you have a tender heart and a gentle soul," he says. "It's not in your nature to hate. At least, not forever, I hope."

"You hope?"

He waves a hand in dismissal, but there's a stiffness to the motion that I can't ignore. If not for the darkness surrounding us, I'd have a better idea if I'm imagining it or not.

"I'll wait as long as it takes for you to forgive me," he says.

"Don't hold your breath."

A smile takes over, and the whites of his teeth penetrate the dimly lit space. "I won't."

"Hayden, please. I need you to take this seriously. I can't have sex with you while my emotions are a mess."

And while I'm pissed about this tattoo.

"Fine."

I squint at him in suspicion. "You gave in too quickly."

"No, I didn't. I already told you that I'm not above seducing you, and that's what I plan to do, starting tomorrow. Now, if you've covered everything on your agenda, I'm going to bed. Our flight leaves early in the morning."

He walks to the bed and pulls back the comforter to settle on the mattress, facing the ceiling. "Come here."

I stay rooted to the spot. "I'm not going."

He remains still but centers his gaze on me. I nearly

flinch at the cold, hard determination within. "I'm not in the mood for games. If you don't get into this bed in the next ten seconds, I'm going to come after you. And when I catch you, you'll be sorry."

With a nonchalance I don't feel, I roll my eyes and make my way to the bed. After crawling onto the mattress to take up my spot next to Hayden, I lie on my side, facing him. "You're an asshole."

"Calista..."

I squeeze my eyes shut, not only to signal my intent to sleep but also to avoid his death glare. Even without me looking at him, I can still feel it burning into my skin. This entire evening has been one giant battle of wills, and now that it's died down, I have time to reflect on it. Unfortunately, I can't stay awake long enough to do anything except mentally reaffirm my stance on this so-called vacation.

I'm not going.

~

I'M GOING.

Hayden woke me up this morning and made good on his threat: he tossed me over his shoulder and carried me to the front door. He only stopped to wrap me in his trench coat, and that was after I shrieked about my inappropriate attire and how I didn't want to be seen in my pajamas.

He pulls sharply on the collar and fastens all of the buttons until I'm covered from my neck to my knees. "I warned you."

"I didn't think you'd actually haul my ass out in the freezing cold."

"I didn't want to, but if that's the only way to move you, then so be it. Are you ready to cooperate?"

I glare at him in answer.

"Have it your way. I have the rope in my pocket, if necessary."

Hayden reaches for me with a speed too quick for me to react. With a grunt, I land on his shoulder, my hair dangling on either side of my face. The skin of my tattoo smarts, and cheeks burn, not just from embarrassment but from outrage. I lift my leg to knee him in the chest, and he slams his arm across the backs of my thighs, preventing me.

Then he swats my ass.

"Enough, Calista. This is happening. If you try to hit me or decide to scream for help, I'll have you bound and gagged so fast it'll make your head spin. Got it?"

I sniff with indignation. It's the best I can manage with my pride in tatters and my ass stinging. My hair sways back and forth with each of his steps, and I don't bother removing it from my face. I'm grateful it covers my mortified expression, even if the staff in the building knows my identity.

Hayden eventually deposits me in the car waiting outside, and I scramble across the leather seats, eager to put some distance between us. He climbs in after me, amusement brightening his gaze.

"Put on your seat belt, Callie."

"I will when I'm good and ready." I insert the metal clasp into the buckle. "Now, I'm ready."

He shakes his head, his lips twitching. "You're so stubborn."

Once the driver steers the vehicle onto the road, I stare out the window and watch the city pass by, sullen and unable to enjoy the view. The occasional honk of horns is the only thing that breaks the silence. After a few minutes, Hayden speaks again.

"I know you're upset with me, but in time, you'll understand why I had to do this."

I remain quiet, refusing to respond or even look at him.

He blows out a breath. "How long do you plan on acting like this?"

"Like what? A woman who's been kidnapped?" I snap.

"Kidnapped is a strong word."

"What else do you call it when a man forcibly grabs someone and shoves them in a car bound for an unknown destination?"

He blows out a breath, and I catch him running a hand through his hair from the corner of my eye. "You can choose to view it that way, or you could see it as me saving you."

"I can't just run away from my problems." I give him a pointed look. "Isn't that what you told me, to quit running?"

"This is different. Besides, I'm not a stranger to you. I'm the person who will put your welfare above everyone's, even my own."

I finally turn to look at him. His gaze finds mine, a storm of emotions churning inside me. His eyes mirror the turmoil in my own. We might be at an impasse again, caught between our conflicting desires, but I never expected to see regret from him. It's quick, no more than a flash. However, it gives me hope.

Maybe Hayden does understand what he's putting me through. If he can sympathize, then he might be reasoned with.

All I have to do is bide my time.

CHAPTER 16

C alista

AN EIGHT-HOUR FLIGHT IS LONG, BUT WHEN YOU TRAVEL ON A private jet, you don't tend to notice.

Except I do. Hayden's next to me, overwhelming me with his intense energy. His thigh brushes mine every so often, and he asks me if I'm all right every half hour. I want to be irritated with his attentiveness, but I can't because I'm tired.

Of everything.

The jet's engines rumble, creating a continuous hum, and it isn't long before I'm slumped in the plush seat, staring out the window through heavy-lidded eyes. Sleep drags me under until the only things I'm aware of are the air conditioning periodically sweeping over my cheeks and the man beside me.

I doubt there'll ever be a time when I can't feel Hayden's presence.

This is the reason I don't immediately release a scream when he grabs my hips and shifts me onto his lap.

"Shh, baby, I've got you," he whispers into my hair.

He gently pushes my cheek to his chest and rests his chin on my head, keeping his arms around my waist. The scent of his cologne, both comforting and familiar, surrounds me while the heat of his body eases into my muscles, relaxing me. I instinctively snuggle closer, burrowing my face in the curve of his neck.

I can hate myself for that show of vulnerability later. Right now, I've entered into a state of mind that's free from turmoil. The tension between us earlier is nonexistent as he traces soothing patterns along my lower back and his heartbeat reverberates against my ear.

Hayden may not want to love me, but I'm pretty sure I love him.

~

THE JOLTING OF THE PLANE JARS ME AWAKE.

I open my eyes as panic sets in, only to find myself held securely against Hayden's chest, his arms tight around my waist.

"You're fine," he murmurs in my ear. "We just landed."

The haze of sleep lifts, and the uncertainty of the situation creeps back in. I shift slightly, trying to extricate myself from his hold. In response, he tightens his grip on me.

"You can let go now," I say.

"I can, but I won't."

The stewardess, who I didn't know was there this entire trip, makes her way down the aisle. "Allow me to welcome you to your destination, Mr. & Mrs. Cole."

Hayden tenses behind me. I open my mouth to correct

her but immediately press my lips together when he digs his fingers into my thigh. I give him a sickly-sweet smile to communicate my displeasure at his high-handedness.

"Thank you," he says to the woman with a polite nod. Then he leans forward, whispering in my ear, loud enough for her to hear. "You can let go now, honey."

"No problem, darling."

I shove off his chest hard enough to cause him to grunt and get into a standing position. My grin is indicative of how petty I am. But it fades the second my bare feet touch the floor. I'd forgotten I'm only wearing my pajamas underneath Hayden's coat. My face blazes with embarrassment.

As if nothing is out of the ordinary, Hayden rises smoothly, unfazed, adjusting his rumpled shirt. The one I cuddled against for nearly eight hours. He meets my gaze, his glinting with humor. I want to smack the smug look off his face.

He leans close, brushing his lips against the shell of my ear. "Play nice."

"Play fair."

"Never."

He retrieves his suitcase, takes my hand, and leads me down the aisle. I paste a smile on my face for the crew members as we leave the jet and get into a nondescript car. This time, Hayden drives.

I settle into the passenger's seat and fasten my seat belt before he can order me to. Then I stare out the window, watching the colorful scenery go by without actually seeing it.

We drive for over two hours before reaching a quiet marina. Hayden parks the car and gets out without saying a word to me. Left with no other choice, I follow him, hugging my arms around my middle, silently fuming. There's a gentle breeze in the air, coming off the water just ahead, but the warm pavement under my bare feet has me wanting to remove his coat.

I don't, refusing to expose my pajamas. Just like with the tattoo, I won't give Hayden the satisfaction of knowing his actions have upset me.

At the end of a long dock sits a sleek motorboat. A man with a straw hat, hula shirt, and khaki shorts reclines in the driver's seat. His snoring halts the second Hayden clears his throat.

"Mr. And Mrs. Cole," the man greets. "Right on schedule. I'm Mateo."

His gaze quickly travels over Hayden, but when it lands on me, he squints. Whether it's in confusion or judgment, I can't tell.

I bite my lip to refrain from rolling my eyes at both the false identity and the fact that Mateo won't stop staring. Hayden gives the man a look of warning, which does the trick.

The boat's engine comes to life while Hayden climbs into the boat and sets down his suitcase. Then he turns back to offer me a hand. I take it but quickly retract my arm to step past him and occupy a seat near the back. If he's bothered by my aloofness, he doesn't show it. As usual, Hayden remains poised and in control.

Mateo steers us out into the open water. My eyelids drift shut as the ocean air whips through my hair and grazes my face. It's refreshing in a way I hadn't anticipated. When I open my eyes, I find Hayden staring at me, a peculiar expression on his face. Before I can ask him about it, he schools his features.

"That's it," Mateo says, pointing straight ahead. "La casa del mar."

I follow the direction he's indicating, and my eyes widen at the sight. It's a small, lush island, enclosed by emerald-tipped palms and surrounded by azure waves. I guess Hayden wasn't lying about that.

We pull up to what appears to be a private dock, and Mateo secures the boat before jumping up to assist us. "Can I take your bag, sir?"

Hayden shakes his head. Mateo frowns, but his expression morphs into excitement when Hayden hands him a crisp bill.

"Thank you, Mr. Cole," he says, holding out a set of keys. "I'll bring the house cleaner twice a week, but if you need an additional visit, please phone the manager of the vacation home and I'll come back the next morning. Your groceries will be delivered every other day unless you specify otherwise. You can find all of the other information in the folder sitting on the kitchen counter. As always, it's a pleasure to serve you." He stops and looks at me. "And you too, Mrs. Cole."

Hayden and I offer our thanks before he's helping me out of the boat and up a winding path lined with palm trees and bushes dotted with various flowers. At the top sits a beach house that could feature in a magazine. It has huge windows overlooking the ocean, a deck that wraps around the entire building, and an airy, open-concept interior visible through the large glass doors.

We step inside, and cool air brushes my cheeks, a welcome reprieve from the heat. I quickly shed Hayden's coat and drape it over my arm.

"This is beautiful," I whisper. These words are the first I've spoken to Hayden in hours.

"I'm glad you like it."

There's a thread of relief in his tone that takes me by

surprise. This man kidnapped me and brought me here but is concerned with my opinion of the place?

"Have you been here before?" I ask.

Hayden shakes his head. "I researched it extensively. Believe it or not, this place was difficult to find. Considering what they charge, you'd think they'd advertise it more heavily." He shrugs. "I guess the exclusivity comes with the price."

"Hmm. Well, I'm going to look around, unless you have a problem with that?"

"No. This property is secure. I made sure of that before we arrived."

My lips thin. He probably had cameras and other safety measures put in place. Not only to ensure my protection but to make sure I stay put.

I give him a nod and wander off to explore my newfound prison. He watches me go with a hint of reluctance but doesn't try to stop me. Smart man. After everything that's happened over the last couple of days, I'm like a powder keg, ready to blow up at the tiniest spark.

I trail my fingers along the walls and over the furniture as I walk from room to room, each of them decorated in a breezy, coastal style made up of beiges and blues. The floor-to-ceiling windows in the master bedroom provide a breathtaking view of the ocean, and the bathroom is fit for a king. However, I'm quick to leave the beautiful space. I have no doubt Hayden means for us to sleep together here, and that's not something I want to acknowledge fully just yet.

In an office toward the rear of the house, I pause beside a reading nook. It's inviting. With a cushioned window seat the size of a twin bed and several fluffy pillows, I flop down onto it.

Three out of the four walls in this room are filled with bookshelves. My curiosity has me jumping to my feet to examine the available titles. There's an eclectic mix of contemporary fiction, nonfiction, classics, and even a few children's books. I run my fingers over the leather-bound spines, smiling to myself.

My smile fades when Hayden's presence washes over me.

"There are a few things we need to discuss," he says without preamble. I stiffen at his tone. It's all business, militant even. "I want to lay out the rules."

I turn to face him and cross my arms. "Rules?"

"Yes," he says. "You're free to enjoy the house and the beach during the day, but I don't want you outside at night."

Irritation fizzles along my skin, but I hold my tongue and gesture for him to continue.

"Don't try to leave the property without me."

"What do you think I'm going to do, Hayden? Start swimming and hope I make it without drowning first? I'm not an idiot."

"I never said you were. I don't want you trying to sneak aboard the boat when our groceries are delivered." He fixes me with a hard stare. "I've already talked to the staff, and they won't help you. Don't act like you haven't considered it."

"Of course I have, but it's not like I expected them to follow through. Besides, I don't have any money or a cell phone. Or *clothes*." I practically spit the last word. "Those are kind of necessary to travel."

"Look, I just don't want there to be any surprises while we're here. I hate them."

"Fine," I say, my voice tight. "Anything else?"

He doesn't answer me for a full minute. Maybe even longer. When he does, his gaze softens, turning as beautiful as the ocean just outside. "Try to enjoy yourself, Callie. I don't want you to be miserable while we're here."

I give him an incredulous look. "You can't be serious."

He takes a step forward, as though to reach out and touch me, but stops when I narrow my gaze. He releases a sigh of defeat that pricks my heart. "I'll see you at dinner."

I give him a curt nod and turn my attention to the window, dismissing him. The waves just outside gently ebb and flow right now, but they have the capacity to grow in strength and drown someone. That's my relationship with Hayden. Sometimes it's beautiful and other times it threatens to kill me.

That thought fills me with sadness and anger in equal measure. I wrap my arms around my middle and stare out of the window as if a solution can be found in the sands below. I press my forehead against the glass, tears burning behind my eyelids.

How am I going to get through this without losing my mind?

CHAPTER 17

C alista

THE SUN IS HIGH WHEN I FINALLY END MY PITY-PARTY AND wander outside, happy to leave Hayden behind indoors. He glanced at me when I walked past him in the living room. He'd been typing furiously on his laptop until I entered the room, but he remained quiet and motionless until I reached the door.

Following the sandy path down to a secluded stretch of beach, I take a deep breath of the salty air, and some of the tension leaves my shoulders. For the first time since I arrived, my body starts to relax. There's a serenity in this place that I'm not immune to, regardless of my personal issues.

And there are many.

I keep walking along the white sandy shore until the water covers my toes. It's cooler than I thought, given the sweltering heat brushing my skin. Shielding my eyes from the sun's brutal rays, I stand there with the waves slapping against my legs until my skin starts to protest.

I head over to the cabana I spotted on my way here. Nestled between a group of palm trees near the shoreline, the structure is covered in shade. A swinging bench is suspended from the ceiling, similar in style to the reading nook inside the library.

After settling onto the plush seat, I push off the floor with both feet, gently rocking as I gaze out at the sparkling water. The sound of the rolling waves mingles with the rustling palm leaves above me, creating a peaceful atmosphere.

Leaning back against the cushions, I close my eyes and let the gentle motion of the swing soothe me. My mind remains blissfully quiet and I lose track of time. Which doesn't matter since I have nowhere else to go.

"Calista."

At the sound of Hayden calling my name, I jolt awake. The swing is still, except for my sudden movement, and the sun is much lower in the sky. I blink away the fog of sleep and look up at him. He towers over me with the remaining sunlight outlining his body, casting him in an orange glow.

He looks like an angel, ethereal and otherworldly. The comparison brings little comfort. Before he fell, Lucifer was an angel too.

I sit up slowly. "What is it?" I ask, unable to keep the suspicion from my voice.

If he notices, he doesn't show it. His face remains placid. "Dinner's ready." My stomach rumbles at the mention of food, and the side of his mouth lifts into a half-smile. "Come on."

He extends a hand and I hesitate to take it. I'm still

emotionally wary of this man. He's keeping me under his control, forcing me to depend on him for everything.

Food.

Shelter.

Fucking underwear.

"You need to eat," he says. "Don't make me repeat myself, Callie."

With a sigh of frustration, I rise from the swing. He lowers his offered hand, but not without his eyes flashing some intense emotion that could either be anger or pain. I'm not sure.

Guilt tries to take over as I follow Hayden back to the house, but I'm quick to suppress it. We reach the patio where a candlelit table waits. He pulls out my chair and I sit down, hyperaware of his proximity. Of his every movement. I'm in tune with this man in a way I didn't think was possible.

"Seafood linguine," he says, taking his seat and lifting the lid of the serving tray. "I believe this is one of your favorites."

"It is."

The flames from the candles flicker, stirred by a gentle breeze, and the shadows dance on Hayden's features. I could hate him for being so beautiful. So irresistible.

He serves us both, heaping our plates with pasta, shrimp, scallops, and lobster, all covered in a white wine sauce. I grab my fork, trying to refrain from digging into the food like a seagull that's found a bagel.

"Eat, Callie. I know you're starving."

I twirl some linguine with my fork and take a bite. The delicious flavors have my eyes fluttering shut. He was right; this is definitely a meal I love. A little moan escapes me. My eyes fly open, and I bite my lip to keep from making any other noises.

But the damage has been done.

Hayden stares at me with his fork suspended in the air and his eyes focused solely on my mouth, as if he's about to lunge for me. And fuck me on this table.

I drop my gaze. A flush works its way onto my cheeks that has nothing to do with the warm temperature. "This is really good. Thank you."

"I'm glad you like it." His voice is guttural but strained, as if he's being strangled. "You can relax. I'm not going to touch you."

Despite his promise, I can't bring myself to believe him. He openly stares at me with a look of hunger, and I don't have the courage to call him out on it. The last time I did, it was useless. If anything, he made me all the more flustered.

We eat in silence for several minutes. In that time, I eat enough pasta to fall into a carb coma and enough wine to feel invincible. I glare at Hayden, wondering if this was his plan all along.

"Why are you looking at me like I just kicked a puppy?" he asks.

"Because I feel good right now."

His brows gather. "And that's a bad thing?"

"Yes."

"This ought to be good," he mutters. Then at a normal volume he says, "Would you care to explain yourself?"

I take a deep breath to steady my nerves. The wine has loosened my tongue—not that it needed much help to begin with—and I need to be careful.

"Feeling good isn't the issue. It's the source." I give him a pointed look. "The lovely dinner, the wine, hell, even the ambiance...it's all from you."

He picks up his wineglass and takes a sip, as if mulling over my words. "And that's a problem?"

"Yes."

"Why?"

"Because of the power dynamic here." I gesture between us. "You have all of the control...what I eat, where I go, everything. My happiness completely depends on what you provide. So even when I feel good, I owe it to you."

I pause, taking a big gulp of wine to bolster my courage. "I can't deny that I appreciate all of this, but real happiness requires freedom and choice. Right now, I don't have either."

Hayden's expression hardens. He slowly takes another drink from his wineglass, regarding me with a detachment that I find unnerving. "I understand what you're saying, but I'm not going to change my mind."

Frustration snakes its way through me and leaks into my words, making them tremble. "You're no better than a dictator."

He scoffs. "Don't be so dramatic. I'm not imprisoning you. I'm protecting you. When this is all over, you can be as free as a bird. *My* little bird."

The way he says it reminds me of the night I gave myself to him. Before I knew he was a stalker, before I knew he'd take over my life.

Before I fell in love with him.

I rise to my feet. "You should trust me enough to know that I'd never knowingly put myself at risk."

Hayden sets his glass down with a thud, his eyes flashing. "None of this will matter if you die!"

He slams his palms on the table as he rises to his feet, making me jump. He leans forward, his nostrils flaring with his anger, his voice a low growl. "I've said this more than once, and tonight it'll be for the last time. I'll do whatever it takes to keep you safe, even if you fucking hate me for it."

Without another word, he turns and strides to the door to disappear inside. My legs shake until I'm forced to sink back into the chair. I stare after him in a daze, alone and trembling from the intensity of our conversation. *Argument* is more accurate.

I wish I felt better about standing up to Hayden, but the only thing left behind from the heated exchange is pain. My heart aches, sitting heavily in my chest as though perched on my rib cage. When I uncurl my fingers from being tightly fisted, I stare down at the crescent-shaped indentations on my palms, red and stinging. The discomfort will pass, but this friction with Hayden?

If he continues to clip my wings, I may not be able to fly...but I'll run.

For good this time.

CHAPTER 18

H ayden

I STORM TO THE OFFICE AND SLAM THE DOOR BEHIND ME. After throwing myself into the plush leather seat, I reach for my laptop and fire it up. The screen comes to life. Too restless to sit there and wait for it to complete its process, I pick up my cell phone and unlock it to call Zack.

If Calista won't take the danger seriously, then I have no choice but to prove it to her.

"El Capitan," the hacker greets, his voice chipper. "What can I do for you?"

"I want an update on Calista's case."

"First of all, I couldn't find any dirt on her father. If he had any shady deals, they've been buried so deep that I won't be able to locate them without a clue or place to start. Secondly, the package that was sent to Miss Green was rerouted several times before it ended up with the final courier. Whoever sent it didn't want anyone to know its origins."

I blow out a breath. "Damn it!"

"I feel you. I even contacted Sebastian to have a 'friendly chat' with the delivery guy and he didn't know anything about the box or where it came from. He's a dead end."

"What about the note inside?"

Zack grumbles. "For the record, 'Will wett ink ken?' is a stupid riddle."

"Did it stump you?"

"Not exactly. I started with the phrase itself. 'Ken' is commonly used in Scotland as 'to know.' Will wet ink know? Know what? That's the question. Duh. I researched various uses for ink, the different types of materials used for it throughout history, and even went as far as to test the ink used on the note itself."

"And nothing?"

"Right," he mumbles, his frustration leaking into his voice. "Then I took each word and weighed them individually. 'Wett' is spelled incorrectly, and I believe it's on purpose, which led me to rearranging the letters to form words and phrases. Turns out to be bullshit. I mean, did they really send a lullaby as a death threat?"

I tense in my chair, ready to end the call as my instincts urge me to return to Calista. All I can think about is her life in danger, yet hearing Zack discuss it has my insides churning with fear and rage. I force my muscles to relax until I'm reclining in the seat.

Zack continues on, oblivious to my turmoil. "'Will wett ink ken' spells out '*Twinkle Twinkle*.' It was written by Jane Taylor, who was born in 1783 and died in 1824. Don't worry, general, I looked into the dates, and nothing. Anyway, the lyrics stem from a 19th century poem that's most likely another dead end. I—"

"Wait!" My shout startles Zack into silence, while my thoughts churn loudly inside my head like bombs detonating. "Twinkle twinkle, little star," I say, my voice barely above a whisper as a realization hits me. It solidifies when I picture the pill in my work desk, the one with a starburst in the center. "The date-rape drug has a star on it."

"Hot damn," Zack says. "I'll go back over the list of pharmaceutical companies with this information in mind. This gives me a better timeline of when this drug compound hit the streets." He pauses and then breaks through my musings with a small cough when I remain quiet. "I'll get right on this, sir."

"Thank you."

"Talk to you soon."

I hang up the phone, staring into the distance. Whoever sent that note to Calista hasn't only confirmed my suspicion that the cases are connected. This person made sure I fucking know it. And that they're responsible for the delivery.

Along with my mother's death.

Given the fact that they specifically sent it to Calista tells me they want me to know she's gotten their attention. This is more than a scare tactic, it's a warning.

My decision to bring her here, literally kicking and protesting, was the right call. I've always known in my gut that my choices concerning Calista's safety were extreme, maybe even irrational at times, but now? I'm completely justified.

I lock my phone's screen, toss it on the desk, and get to my feet. My thoughts about Calista propel me forward, to be by her side. I need to hold her, even if it's only for a moment.

My steps echo in the hallway, the heels of my shoes tapping out a cadence that's almost militant. I certainly feel like I'm at war. Not only with this unknown threat, but with Calista herself.

I approach the master bedroom and grab the handle to open the door. The room is dimly lit, with the glow of a seashell lamp casting a warm, inviting light. My gaze immediately finds Calista standing just inside the bathroom, a light blue towel wrapped around her body. Her hair is damp from the shower, and there are droplets of water scattered over her chest because of it. When she turns to face me, they sparkle like diamonds, drawing my gaze to her breasts.

Lips parting on a gasp, she takes a step back. "What's wrong?"

"Hey," I say, softening my voice. "I didn't mean to scare you. I wanted to check and make sure you're all right."

Her eyes turn to molten gold, piercing me where I stand. I resist the need to grab her and pull her into my arms. God, just the sight of her...

She straightens her shoulders and holds my stare, a mixture of wariness and curiosity. "I appreciate that, but I'm fine."

We lapse into silence, me studying Calista and her judging me. I rake a hand through my hair, trying to rid myself of the terror that grips me whenever I think of her being hurt.

"I just finished talking to the person I hired to decipher the note," I say. "They confirmed it's a death threat, not just a warning."

The flush from the hot shower leaves her cheeks. "Are you sure?"

I nod. "It translates to 'star,' which is the symbol on the pills that my mother took when she overdosed."

"Hayden..." She swallows, and the fluttering of her throat draws my attention. She's delicate, so fragile. "Now what?"

"Zack is going to keep searching for answers."

"Why would someone want to hurt me?"

"If I knew, I would've already dealt with them." I lean against the doorframe and cross my arms to keep from snatching her to me. "That doesn't mean I won't. Until then..."

She averts her gaze. "Until then, we'll stay here."

"Callie—"

"I know why you're doing this, but it doesn't make it right."

"Right or wrong, I can't lose you."

She sighs, her shoulders slumping. "Only you can make love dysfunctional."

"Do you have any idea what you do to me?" My voice carries threads of my desperation for her, but I can't find the energy to care.

She clutches the towel tighter, her fingers digging into the fluffy material as she shakes her head, still looking down. I walk right up to her, slide my hand around the back of her neck and force her to look me in the eyes as I bare my soul to her.

"All I see is you. All I want is you. When I'm not with you, I can't think. You've fucking wrecked me, but I don't care. Not if it means I get to have you."

Her breath hitches, and her pupils dilate, revealing the fear, anger, and confusion. Underneath it all is a spark of desire. I want to fan it until it's a flame that burns brightly, evolving into an inferno. She wants this as much as I do, regardless of how much she tries to resist.

"Hayden..." She raises her hands to rest her palms on my chest. "I can't do this right now."

"Don't fight this. Don't fight *us*."

CHAPTER 19

H ayden

A SINGLE TEAR ESCAPES TO TRAIL DOWN HER CHEEK. I LEAN IN
to capture it with my lips, tasting the saltiness of it on my
tongue. She shivers against me and curls her fingers into the
material of my shirt. Does she want to pull me closer or
push me away?

I inhale slowly as I struggle with the primal urge to take
what I want. My intellect suggests that I wait. It's only a
matter of time until she's pregnant. Knowing her the way I
do, carrying my baby will soften her attitude toward me.
And her protective instincts will kick in once she realizes
her condition. That should make her more likely to adhere
to my safety instructions.

My hands tremble with my need for her as I retract
them. She wraps her arms around her middle, looking small
and vulnerable. And she is.

"I have something for you," I say. I wait for her to give me a sarcastic remark about the tattoo. Surely she's noticed it by now. Calista might be stressed, but she's not out of touch with reality.

She jerks up her head, searching my gaze. "You do?"

I nod, ignoring my twinge of disappointment when she fails to mention her tattoo. "I've been waiting for the right moment to give it to you, but I think you need it now."

She watches me as I walk over to my suitcase and unzip it. I return to Calista with the velvet box clutched in my hand. Her eyes widen when she sees it, but she says nothing.

"This isn't a traditional gift, since it was yours to begin with," I say. "But I know you want it back, regardless." I open the box to reveal the pearl necklace inside. "They're all present and accounted for. Sixty-four in total."

Calista inhales sharply and covers her mouth with a shaking hand. "Is that...?" When I nod, the tears that were glistening in her eyes begin to fall. She sniffles and wipes her cheeks, but doesn't reach for the necklace.

I extend my arm, putting the jewelry closer to her, urging her to take it. "I'm the one who broke it, so I had to be the one who restored it."

When she remains frozen, I carefully lift the pearls from the box and step behind her. She trembles as I brush her hair over her shoulder. I lean down and press a kiss to the side of her neck, taking advantage of her shocked state. Once I fasten the clasp, I take her shoulders and slowly turn her to face me.

"I'm sorry I took this from you."

Her gaze flits to mine. "Hayden Bennett, is that a sincere apology? I don't think I've ever heard one before."

I glare at her, but the look carries no heat. "Don't get used to it."

"I wouldn't dream of it." She runs her fingers over the

strand, and her lips tilt up in a small smile. "Thank you. I can't tell you what this means to me. My dad gave this to me."

At the mention of her father, my gut clenches. "That makes it special."

She nods, her expression turning thoughtful. "How did you know the exact number of pearls?"

"The night I took the necklace, I counted them." When she scrunches her forehead in confusion, I shrug. "It worked out in the end."

"Hmm," she says, the sound threaded with doubt. "It surprises me that you counted them to begin with."

"I'll always take care of what's important to you, down to memorizing inconsequential details."

I reach out and trace the curve of the necklace, watching the flickering of her pulse quicken. She inhales sharply but doesn't pull away. Emboldened, I slide my hand to grasp the nape of her neck beneath the string of pearls. Our gazes lock and the air fizzles with sexual tension.

And emotional connection.

"You mean everything to me," I say. "No matter how much we argue, that'll never change."

"I'm finally starting to believe that."

Before I can respond, she rises on her toes and brushes her lips over mine. It's over way too soon as far as I'm concerned, but I refrain from grabbing her. Calista hardly ever shows me affection, and I never want to do anything that'd discourage her from doing so.

It doesn't take a genius to know that shoving my cock in her mouth might piss her off.

My fingers tighten on her neck as I repress the urge to kiss her, to finish what she started. What she just did was a fucking tease that has my pulse racing and dick hardening. My sexual frustration is at an all-time high.

Calista's eyes flutter open, her eyes swirling with emotion. "Thank you for the necklace. I've really missed it."

Her pulse thrums against my fingertips, quickening with her confession. The pearls lie still against my hand, cool and smooth to the touch, but the heat from Calista's skin has already begun to warm them. The flush that now tinges her cheeks isn't from gratitude.

She's affected by me.

It's time to use that to my benefit. Which will end up satisfying her as well.

"You're welcome," I say.

"Since you're in a generous mood, I'd like to ask for another gift."

"You never have to ask me to make you come."

Her jaw drops. "That's not what I meant."

"That's a shame."

"I wanted to ask for some clothes," she says. When I shake my head, she frowns at me. "Why not?"

"You know why. I told you to pack, and you refused. This is the consequence of your actions. Or inaction, to be exact. I don't know how many times I have to prove to you that I mean what I say."

Calista wrenches from my hold, her gaze narrowed and her chest heaving. The towel slides down an inch, and I follow the movement with my gaze. She hitches up the material with a huff when she notices my focus shift downward.

"You're infuriating," she says, anger brightening the hazel of her eyes. "This is completely unreasonable."

I fold my arms. "Life is about choices. You've already made one, and now it's time for another. It's up to you whether you wear your pajamas every day or nothing at all. I suppose that towel is also an option."

Her dainty nostrils flare right before she rips the material from her body. I blink in surprise. But also due to the vision that stands before me.

Seeing Calista naked would bring any man to his knees.

I pointedly look at the gauze covering her tattoo before meeting her gaze. It flares with the heat of her anger, and she lifts a brow. I see the challenge she's thrown my way and nearly smile.

My little bird isn't mentioning her tattoo on purpose. Interesting...

"You're right," she snaps. "I do have a choice."

"I like this decision."

She takes a step back, putting herself out of my reach. "I'll bet you do. Is there any point in me sleeping in another room, or are you going to..."

"Pick the lock? Yes, I will. You're sleeping with me. That's *not* a choice."

"Figures."

Calista simmers with fury. It's in the way she yanks on the comforter and then the sheets. She punches the pillow several times while muttering to herself before settling on the mattress and covering her body from view.

I don't bother hiding my grin. Her fiery spirit is one of the things that I love about her.

"Good night, Callie."

"Go to hell, Hayden."

She turns off the lamp, plunging the room into darkness, with my laughter echoing around us.

CHAPTER 20

C alista

Revenge is a dish best served cold. And naked.

Unless you count a pearl necklace as attire, which I don't.

After my conversation with Hayden last night, I came to a conclusion. If he feels the need to deny me clothes, then no clothes it is.

I don't bother retrieving my pajama set from the dryer. Instead, I parade through the house the next day as if nothing is out of the ordinary, ignoring the elegant script on my hip.

"Morning," I say, waltzing into the kitchen with my hair down.

Hayden pauses with his coffee mug halfway to his mouth. His gaze travels the length of my body in a slow perusal that has my skin pricking. By the time he returns his focus to my face, I feel like I've been caressed all over. I fight back a blush.

"What's for breakfast?" I ask.

"Pussy."

I make a face at him, even though my insides quiver. Giving him my back—which isn't the smartest decision when dealing with Hayden—I open the refrigerator and grab the orange juice. After retrieving a cup and pouring myself a glass, I sit across from him at the dining table.

"What's your plan for today?" I ask.

I watch Hayden over the rim of my glass, trying to gauge his mood. He was definitely strung tight when I walked into the room, but that was expected. Now that he knows what game I'm playing, he's leaning back in his chair, his posture relaxed. I'm not naïve enough to think he won't try something to gain the upper hand. I just wish I knew what it was.

He blows out a breath and shakes his head, setting his coffee down. "I have a lot of case files to go through."

"Oh, okay. I didn't realize you were still working."

"I have to work remotely, or I won't have a job when I get back."

"Right."

A twinge of disappointment snakes through me, and I bite my lip. I don't want to depend on him for anything, but the idea of spending day after day alone in this place makes me shudder.

"Stop biting your lip," he says.

I obey, not wanting to provoke more than I already have.

"Wait here."

I watch him get to his feet and leave the room, my forehead wrinkled in confusion. He returns with a large package, complete with a red bow. After setting it on the table, he pushes it toward me, his gaze earnest.

"For you."

"Another present?" I ask. When he nods, I finger the pearls at my throat. "But you already gave me one."

"Is there a rule about the number of gifts a man can give?"

I shake my head. "I guess not."

"Open it, Callie."

Hesitation rises in me, colliding with excitement. I don't trust the motivations behind Hayden's gifts. It's obvious he's trying to soothe the rift between us with material things, since he refuses to give in on the main source of contention. If I accept this, does that mean I'm telling him I agree with the way he's handled everything?

I glance at Hayden, finding his expression even. Except for the sparkle of eagerness in his gaze. It warms my heart a little. With a sigh, I untie the bow and unwrap the box. Nestled inside is a sleek laptop. From the looks of it, top of the line and the latest model.

"What's this for?" I ask.

"College. You can use it to register and for the classes when they begin. I gave you my word that I'd support you in that. Remember?"

I drop my gaze, tracing the metal case with my index finger. "I do."

"You don't like it." His voice is flat, hard. "Is that the problem?"

"I love it."

"Then what's wrong?"

Having this laptop would make my time here easier to get through. By giving me access to school, he's not only keeping his promise, he's giving me a way to connect to other people beyond this island. But using this gift feels like an acceptance of my situation.

"This is a very thoughtful gift," I say slowly, keeping my gaze downcast. "And you're right, having this laptop would really help me. But...I just...I can't take it."

Even though I'm not staring directly at him, I catch the stiffening of his body. He remains quiet, and the tension in the room builds with every passing second. It has me shifting in my seat until I finally dare to glance up at him.

"Why can't you take it?" he asks, his voice dangerously soft.

I gently gnaw on the inside of my cheek, carefully choosing my words. "Because it makes me feel uncomfortable, given our situation."

"Our situation? You mean where I provide everything you could ever possibly want or need?"

"Except clothes," I mutter.

"Mrs. Bennett..."

I nearly wince at the name. And the warning underneath. "For once, can you try to understand where I'm coming from?"

"If you felt about me the way I feel about you, this wouldn't even be a discussion." He rests his forearms against the table, his brows lowered. "You belong to me now. Your needs and wants? I take them seriously. When I deny you, it pains me. Don't you get that? Seeing you upset is the last thing I want."

I flinch at the sincerity in his words. "Hayden, please."

"I'm through discussing it. Throw the laptop into the fucking ocean if you want, but you're not using mine."

He gets to his feet and walks away, leaving me gaping after him.

I'm not sure how long I sit there in stunned silence, but eventually I stand up and head outside. The sun shines brightly as I make my way to the cabana and there's a gentle breeze that kisses my bare skin. Well, except my hip, which I'm covering with my hand. I shake my head at myself. Hayden has won again. Instead of hiding my crotch, I'm protecting my tattoo from the sun because I don't want it to fade.

I curl up on the swing, tuck my legs underneath me, and set the laptop on my thighs. Hayden's hurt expression swims through my vision as I stare blankly at the screen in front of me, unable to focus.

"It's not like he hasn't hurt you," I mutter.

My justification doesn't soothe the guilt, but I refuse to go to him. He and I have different views on reality, and I'm not sure he'll ever see things from my perspective. Right now, there's nothing I can do about that. However, I can choose to keep my promise to take care of myself and my future.

I sigh and power on the computer. It hums and lights up, displaying a picture. Of me. The black-and-white photo that hangs in Hayden's bedroom stares back at me.

"Romantic but creepy," I say to myself. "Pretty much sums up my love life."

Off to the side of the home screen is a bright yellow sticky note. It contains login information. *My* login information. I freeze as a sneaky suspicion works its way through my subconscious.

My fingers slightly tremble as I connect to the WiFi network Hayden set up. This laptop is my only source of communication to anyone outside of this island, but I doubt it'll be that simple. Knowing my stalker, he'll control what I can see and do.

Yahtzee.

"Of course, the only website I can access is the university's," I say with an eye roll. "Well, joke's on you. Harper is a student at Columbia too."

I use the information from the sticky note to access the student log-in and find that my profile is completely filled out. The only thing that's missing is my major and the classes I'll select.

After flopping back on the pillows, I stare at the site, emotions churning in my chest. On one hand, it's very thoughtful that Hayden took the initiative. On the other, it's fucking annoying that he won't let me do things for myself. I'm kind of surprised he didn't pick my class schedule for me.

If he had, I totally would've yeeted this laptop into the ocean.

Choosing to be productive, I sit back up and navigate the website. For over an hour, I go through various course descriptions, as well as the different pathways toward graduation. Before my father's untimely death, I was a communications major.

Is that still something I want to pursue?

I select a mixture of general education courses that sound interesting, along with some core classes that could go either way. Literature, calculus II, sociology, and psychology. I laugh to myself at this. Maybe if I take that class, it'll explain why Hayden's so fucked up.

What does that say about me?

With the registration complete, I go through the student directory and select Harper's name to start up a chat thread. I don't expect her to write back, but it'd be really nice to hear from her if she happens to check her inbox.

> Calista: Hey there! Guess who's registered for the spring semester? :)

After closing the laptop, I set it aside and curl up on the mound of pillows. Between the energy I expended on my decision-making and the lethargy brought on by the afternoon heat, I release a yawn. Sleep tugs at me. It isn't surprising considering it took me a long time to fall asleep last night.

I kept expecting Hayden to seduce me.

With me freshly showered and naked in his bed, it was a rational assumption. However, he surprised me. Yes, he grabbed me and forced my body flush to his, wrapping an arm around my middle so I couldn't escape, but that was it. Unless I count the sweet kiss that he placed on the crown of my head, which I don't.

As I start to drift, my thoughts continue circling around Hayden. I want to share my decision to be a sociology major and my new class schedule with him. I want to know what he thinks, as well as express my excitement about getting back into higher education. Yet something holds me back.

I fall asleep before I come up with a reason.

CHAPTER 21

C alista

I'm brought out of sleep by a simple caress. It's a light pressure on both my ankles before a pair of hands glides up my calves to settle on my thighs. I open my eyes to find Hayden kneeling in front of the swing. His gaze is bright with determination.

I gasp when he yanks my legs apart. "Hayden?" My voice is breathless...and excited?

He leans forward. His palms rest on my inner thighs, holding me in place. To prevent me from denying him.

He keeps his gaze locked on mine as he lowers his head and wraps his lips around my clit. He pulls it into his mouth with the perfect amount of suction, and his tongue swirls around the bit of flesh, making me moan.

His mouth moves against me hungrily, his hands coming up to cup my hips as he pulls me closer. His tongue is relentless in its explorations, devouring me until I groan and squirm beneath him, trying to get even closer. His grip tightens, bruising me in his efforts to keep me still.

He moves up and down, teasing me with gentle strokes and increasing the intensity until I'm panting for more. My fingers curl into fists as I try to hold on to something solid in order to keep from flying away with pleasure. I grip his hair and yank him closer. The added pressure from his mouth has me groaning.

Finally, when I think I can't take any more, he slips two fingers inside me and begins to thrust in time with his mouth's movements. The combination is too much. I cry out as an orgasm slams into me like a tidal wave crashes against shoreline rocks. My whole body shakes uncontrollably while Hayden continues to kiss and lick me until I'm limp with satisfaction.

He presses a kiss to my tattoo before sliding up my body, bringing our faces level once again. His lips hover just inches away from mine, his breath fanning across my skin like a summer breeze before finally pressing against mine in a passionate kiss that leaves me trembling with desire for more.

Then he's gone.

∼

Harper: Hey there, stranger. I'm not sure why you're texting me on the university's messaging system, but it's cool. Here's my schedule. See if we have any classes together. If not, make it happen ;)

Calista: Hi! I'll see you for psychology.

Harper: Awesome. Maybe we'll find out the reason why you're so dick-stracted by Hayden.

Calista: *eye roll* Pot / kettle.

Harper: Haha. True story. Anyway, when are you coming back? I'm not sure if I should ask, but... Any updates on the mystery box?

Calista: Not sure when we'll be home. And not really. Hayden is convinced I'm in danger and that someone's sending me a message. I have no idea why I'm involved. Can I ask a favor?

Harper: Duh. Go for it.

Calista: Can you ask your mom if she's ever come across a drug that has a star symbol on it? Hayden thinks it could be a clue.

Harper: I'll ask her. Okay, I've gotta run. Message me tomorrow. Xoxo

Calista: Will do. Xoxo.

EVERY DAY, I EXCHANGE TEXTS WITH HARPER.

Every day, Hayden sexes me up when I least expect it.

I'm not sure how many more orgasms I can take...said no woman ever. But this constant attention from him is beginning to wear me down emotionally. He's licked my pussy in the cabana, finger-fucked me on the beach, and he ate *me* on the dining room table. He said, "You taste better than any fucking dessert. Sweeter, too."

And those are just the highlights of his seduction crusade.

Back in New York, I told him no sex, and not once has he tried to sleep with me. How am I supposed to be upset with Hayden when he's respecting the boundary that I set?

When I tried to argue that oral sex was included in the rule, he said that I hadn't stipulated it in the verbal contract, therefore he wasn't entitled to adhere to that.

"Lawyers," I mutter to myself, shaking my head at his antics.

The water from the shower continues to pelt against my skin, clearing it of the sand and salt water from my swim earlier. I take my time washing my hair and body, using the solitude to organize my thoughts before I have dinner with Hayden. Immediately, my nipples harden, and heat gathers low in my belly.

Hayden is like a drug. He takes me higher than I've ever been, an out-of-body experience that nothing compares to. Like an addiction, I can't think of him without wanting him, wanting that next hit of ecstasy, that next fix.

I close my eyes and slide my hand between my thighs to stroke my clit. The pleasure is instant, and I clench my teeth, stifling a groan. Hayden ruined me like he said he would. Just the thought of him and I'm aroused, my pussy wet and aching to be filled.

"What are you doing, Callie?"

At the sound of his voice, my finger stills, and I open my eyes. Hayden stands in the doorway, his gaze pinning me where I stand. I open my mouth, and nothing comes out, not even a denial. He's caught me, plain and simple. I yank my arms to my sides.

"Don't stop because of me," he says. "I want to watch."

I gently nibble on my bottom lip, unsure of what to do.

His eyes narrow, his focus completely on my mouth. Then he's striding toward me.

"What did I say about biting your lip?" he snaps.

Hayden's energy pours off of him in waves, full of intensity. He yanks the shower door open and leaves it ajar to step inside, completely clothed. His black slacks and white dress shirt immediately become soaked. I stare at his chest, watching the material become translucent and cling to his skin, outlining the taut muscle underneath.

"What are you doing?" I ask.

He doesn't answer me, but sinks to his knees. After gripping my thighs, he pulls them apart, his breath hissing between his teeth. "Such a pretty pussy. Touch yourself."

His voice is deep, his tone raw, leaving no room for argument. I slowly drag my hand down until it's between my thighs. He leans forward, so close his breath grazes my sensitive flesh, making me squirm. He watches intently, his gaze never wavering from me, and his fingertips dig into my skin with every circular motion.

I release the moan gathering at the back of my throat. Hayden briefly closes his eyes, inhaling, his chest rising.

"Faster," he says.

For once, I'm happy to obey him. I quicken my pace, studying his face as I touch myself. He's so beautiful. On his knees before me, Hayden looks at me as if I'm a goddess and his will is mine to bend.

He smiles. "That's a good girl."

My pussy flutters with his praise, and I groan, my orgasm looming. He presses a kiss on my tattoo, and then on my inner thigh, careful not to disturb me as I bring myself to the edge. After nuzzling my flesh, his breath whispers against my skin.

"Come for me. Hard."

The air rushes out of my lungs in a tiny shriek. When my hips buck against my hand, he presses me hard against the wall, keeping me in place. I come, letting the exquisite sensation wash over me again and again until I'm spent, my head hanging.

Hayden licks his lips. "My turn."

He leans forward and drags his tongue from my entrance up to my clit and back down again, tantalizingly slow so that I feel every bit of it.

"Oh, God," I pant.

"That's not my name." Hayden runs his tongue up my slit again and then nips at my sensitive flesh. A prick of pain has me jerking, but his hands keep me in place. He looks up at me, his eyes smoldering with lust. "Say it."

"Hayden," I whisper.

He groans, the sound muffled by my skin. He moves back to my entrance and thrusts his tongue inside until my legs are shaking. "Again," he commands.

"Hayden." I'm louder this time, my voice more pleading.

His pupils contract, the black shimmering when he shoves two fingers inside me. The sudden penetration wrenches a gasp from me, but my body welcomes it, my pussy gripping him tightly. I grind down on his fingers, trying to create some friction, to get some relief.

"Beg me, Callie."

I part my lips, but nothing comes out except a low wail. I need him to move, to give me what my body is screaming for. He twists his fingers, and I moan.

"I said, beg me."

"Please."

He adds a third finger, stretching and filling me. Then he slides them in and out, driving them deeper and faster each time. But when he puts his mouth on my clit at the same time, I lose it.

I grab his wet hair and shove his face between my legs until I'm feeling that delicious pressure from both inside and out. "Harder," I grit out, digging my nails into his scalp.

For a second, I think I hear him laugh softly at my demand. Then he stops pleasuring me, but only to toss one of my legs over his shoulder. With the new position opening me up to him more, he dives back in, his mouth and fingers fucking me into oblivion.

I come all over his face.

My orgasm leaves me breathless, and it takes a while to recede. During that time, Hayden continues stroking me, slowly guiding me down from the intense high. However, when his gaze finds mine, it bores into me, his pupils blown wide with lust.

"Hayden?"

He rises, his hands sliding up my legs until they reach my hips, his thumbs rubbing circles on my hip bones. He looms over me like a shadow, eclipsing my will until he's in command.

"Kiss me. Taste yourself."

His voice is dark, laced with power. I press my lips to his before swiping my tongue along the seam of his mouth.

He groans and thrusts against me, grinding his cock into my belly. I do this over and over, teasing and languishing until he's shaking with impatience.

He reaches up to grip my jaw and forces my mouth open so he can claim it fully. The taste of me is salty on his tongue as he plunges inside, devouring me. After threading his fingers in my hair, he grips the strands tightly, making me arch into his touch. I wrap my arms around him as he overwhelms me and I sag against him, needing his support to remain standing.

Hayden breaks the kiss, his eyes wild. "Fuck, I can't get enough of you."

"You have me."

"Do I?"

The question has my brows snapping together. He doesn't mean physically. I run my gaze over him, taking in Hayden's yearning for me, his need for my love. Have I truly forgiven him?

"Almost," I say.

He drops his hands and takes a step back. Despite the steam all around us and the warm water hitting my body, I shiver. The iciness is back in his gaze, fighting for dominance against his desire.

"Almost isn't enough," he says.

CHAPTER 22

C alista

HAYDEN MOVES TO LEAVE, BUT I GRAB HIS ARM, HALTING HIM.
He glances down at my hand and then up at me.

"Wait. Please," I whisper. He watches me carefully,
waiting for me to continue. I don't know what to say, so I
blurt out the first thing that comes to mind. "Are you ready
to admit you're in love with me?"

His face is a blank canvas. He considers me, his eyes
slowly traveling over my face before he answers, "Almost."

I rear back, letting go of him. "Point taken."

"Let me know when your 'almost' is a 'yes,' Callie."

I squint up at him. "You too."

Once he's gone, I sink to the floor and hug my knees to
my chest. His willingness to take this at whatever pace I
want is something I hadn't expected. Isn't that enough to
prove he cares about me and wants to move on?

After getting out of the shower and drying off, I walk

into the bedroom wrapped in a fresh towel. I grab my laptop, sit on the bed, and pull up my texting thread with Harper.

> Calista: I think I finally understand what you meant when you said you'd do anything to protect someone you love. If that's who you are and who Hayden is, maybe I need to be more understanding and accepting...
> Anyway, text me when you get this. I need my bff.

Neither Hayden nor Harper talks to me for the next forty-eight hours. By hour forty-nine, I'm ready to beg Hayden and lecture Harper. I won't, but I want to. Instead, I make my way to the office and knock on the door.

Hayden jerks up his head, his gaze brightening with appreciation as it travels over my naked body. "What do you need, Callie?"

"Do you have a minute?" When he nods, I make my way into the room and perch on the edge of the desk. "I need to ask for a favor."

He frowns. "What is it?"

"As I'm sure you know, I've been messaging Harper every day for almost three weeks now, but she hasn't responded for the last two days. I know it's probably nothing, but I'm worried. Her suddenly going quiet on me isn't normal."

"Your friend is anything but quiet."

"Exactly." I cross my legs and place my hands on my lap. "Since you won't let me have my phone—" I stop and give him a frown. "I was wondering if you could reach out and make sure she's okay."

"Give me a second." He retrieves his phone, types out a text to send, and then places it back on his desk. He picks up his pen and jots down a note on his legal pad before looking back at me. "Done."

I smile at him. "Thank you."

The urge to kiss him overcomes me, and I brush my lips over his before I think better of it. His eyes flare, his grip on his pen tightening. When he speaks, his voice is low. "Was there anything else?"

"Nope," I say quickly. Too quickly.

He lifts a brow, a silent inquiry. "I can always tell when you're lying. Tell me what you need."

I press my lips together, biting the inside of my cheek. I can feel Hayden's power beckoning me, pulling the truth out of me. "I'm tired of fighting with you."

The air sizzles with attraction, crackling across my skin. My heart pounds in my ears, the sound drowning out everything else except the man in front of me. Hayden's nostrils flare, and the pen clatters to the desk before he pushes it away.

My lips part, my breath hitching at the hungry look in his eyes. I lean in closer, the need to feel his mouth on mine overwhelming me. I close the distance and press my lips to his. It's a sweet kiss, but I know it's more than that.

I'm finally surrendering to him.

He stands and slides his hands over my waist, then runs them over my thighs before gripping my knees and pulling them apart. A small chime sounds, along with a tiny buzzing noise. I blink at him in a daze as he retrieves his phone. He reads the message, and I can sense the immediate change in him. His body goes taut and a muscle flickers along his jaw.

"What is it?" I ask. When he doesn't answer me, panic builds in my chest. "Hayden?"

He puts the phone away and gives me his full attention. "Your friend is safe."

I wait for an explanation. When Hayden remains silent, warning bells go off in my head. "What aren't you telling me?"

His expression remains blank, but he squeezes my knee. "Don't worry, Callie. Everything is under control."

"What's under control? Hayden, what's going on?"

"Everything is fine."

"You're lying to me."

I lean over to grab his phone, but he stops me by gripping my shoulders. "I just want to talk to her," I say.

"She's resting."

"Convenient."

"Listen to me. She's safe and in good hands."

I jab my finger into his chest. "I swear to God that if you don't tell me what the hell is going on, I'm going to do something crazy."

He stares down at me for a while, his gaze scrutinizing my face. Whatever he sees there causes him to blow out a breath. I brace myself for whatever he's about to tell me.

"Harper has a concussion and a fractured wrist. Even though she was on a crosswalk, it was a hit and run. I can't get any other details on her condition since I'm not family, but she's alive."

"Oh, my God," I say, my words ending in a sob. "I need to go home."

"Callie," he says, his tone gentling, "she's being treated at the best hospital in the city. Trust me. She'll be fine."

I cover my face with my hands, fighting back tears. When I look at him again, I say, "None of this is fine. I need to go home. I have to be there for her. Don't you understand that?"

He shakes his head. "No."

"Hayden! Please, just listen to me—"

"The answer is no." He pockets his cell phone and settles back in the chair. "I hate to do this, Callie, but I won't risk your life."

I slide from the desk to kneel on the floor between Hayden's legs. His gaze widens slightly, but he doesn't move to stop me when I reach for him. I rest my palms on the tops of his thighs and bow my head, the ends of my hair brushing his pants.

"Please," I whisper. "I'll do anything."

"Anything?"

"Yes."

He stops to think, but it doesn't take long. "Forgive me. Not *almost* but completely."

I jerk my head up to look at him. "I'm not a robot. I can't just flip a switch and change my feelings. That's not how emotions work."

He leans down to capture my chin between his thumb and index finger. "You've already forgiven me. If you hadn't, you wouldn't have let me eat that pussy of yours until you drenched my face. If you hadn't forgiven me, you wouldn't be naked and on your knees, ready to be fucked, if that's what I asked for. I want to hear you admit it. Say you forgive me for everything I've done since we first met."

I'm about to deny it, but I stop because he's right. I don't feel the anger I did the day we arrived here. I stare up at him, my bottom lip trembling with the nervous energy racing through me. "Let me be clear, if you don't take me home, I'll hate you. But right now, I'm willing to forgive you for everything, Hayden."

He doesn't give me a triumphant smile like I expect. Instead, he breathes out slowly, as though relieved that a weight has been lifted from him. Before I can ask, he trails a hand down my cheek and along my jaw.

"We'll be gone within the hour." A hint of a grin makes its way onto his mouth when he says, "At least it won't take you long to pack."

CHAPTER 23

C alista

THE PLANE LEVELS OUT AT CRUISING ALTITUDE AS I stare absently out the window. My thoughts are thousands of miles away, consumed with worry about Harper. She's been in the hospital for two days, and I feel so helpless being unable to visit or even talk to her.

A gentle touch on my shoulder makes me flinch. I turn to find Hayden studying me with a look of concern. "You're worrying about your friend again," he says. It's not a question.

I nod, a lump rising in my throat. "I know Harper has her mother, but...I want to be there for her."

Hayden reaches for my hand, his thumb stroking my knuckles in a gentle caress. "We'll be there soon. Everything will be all right."

The tenderness in his voice makes my breath hitch. I

search his face, looking for signs of him placating me, but there are none. His eyes only hold sincerity. "Thank you."

He nods, continuing to stroke my hand. "I know how difficult it's been for you these past weeks, but I never wanted to be your enemy, Callie." His voice is quiet, but that doesn't hide the strain underneath. "My only goal in life is to make you happy."

I give him a wry smile. "As long as it doesn't compromise my safety, right?"

He smiles back at me and cups my cheek. "Right."

The space between us becomes charged with intimacy, and I resist the urge to kiss him. I lean into his palm instead, soaking in the tenderness of the moment.

We race toward home, with Hayden watching me closely. He doesn't yank me onto his lap like last time, but I can tell he wants to. He takes my hand in his, threading our fingers, and he doesn't let go, even when we land.

He leads me from the plane, and the winter air slices through my clothes. Sebastian waits for us next to an idling vehicle, his gaze sharp and assessing. When he takes in my hula shirt, bright orange skirt and sandals, his lips twitch. I make a face at him before burrowing further into Hayden's coat. It was either this outfit from the tourist shop or my birthday suit.

Once Hayden and I are settled in the backseat, he turns to me. "I know you want to see Harper, but I suggest we run home and have you change into clothes that are weather-appropriate. Plus, that'll give you a chance to eat something."

I open my mouth to argue that I'm fine and I don't want to take him up on his suggestion, but then he says, "I need to make sure you're taken care of first, baby."

Shocked into silence, I nod. Hayden never calls me baby

unless he's in a state of emotional overwhelm, and it's never in public. The endearment echoes in my mind, a reminder of how much this man affects me.

Because I love him.

If I didn't, I wouldn't have forgiven him.

After a quick detour to Hayden's penthouse, the hospital looms into view as we turn into the parking lot. Hayden helps me out of the car and places a hand on my back, guiding me inside. I inquire about Harper at the front desk and get her room number.

We step into the elevator, and the sterile hospital smell hits me, making my stomach churn. As if sensing my unease, Hayden pulls me to his side, tucking my body next to his.

"She's fine," he says quietly.

I nod, taking solace in his confidence. However, as we walk down the hall, my anxiety takes over, making my hands shake. When we reach Harper's room, I pause and take a deep breath before pushing open the door.

My usually vibrant and cheerful friend lies motionless in the hospital bed with an IV line hooked up to her arm and a heart monitor beeps steadily, filling the quiet. Until she sees me.

"Calista! You're here!"

I rush over and hug her. With a sniff, I sit on the bed. "Of course I came. How are you feeling?"

"Meh," she says with a shrug. "Honestly, I don't remember anything. One minute I was hauling ass across the street, and the next I'm waking up in here."

"Where's your mom?"

"She'll be here first thing in the morning. I sent her home because she's been here so much that she's getting on the nurses' nerves."

I drop my voice to a whisper. "Is she getting you the good shit?" I flick my gaze to the IV.

Harper bursts out laughing. "I've missed you."

"You too."

"Hey there, Mr. Bennett," Harper says, her voice chipper. "Thanks for bringing *our* girl to visit me."

Hayden steps forward with the side of his mouth quirking up. "Of course, Miss Flynn. Calista cares about you a great deal."

"I'm glad she's here, but I didn't want to interrupt your getaway."

"Family first," he says.

"That's right." Harper tilts her head and looks up at him with her gaze narrowed. "So, let's talk about felonies, Mr. Attorney. I want to know what to do about this asshole who hit me."

He waves a hand. "Go for it."

I watch them chat amicably. The tension leaves my body, and I relax for the first time since I heard Harper had been hospitalized. Hayden answers all of her outrageous "how to break the law without actually breaking the law" questions without giving her any attitude. She even makes him laugh a couple of times. Seeing them together soothes my nerves and makes my heart happy.

When I yawn, Hayden ends the conversation. "I better get Calista to bed," he says, looking at me.

"But—"

He holds up a hand. "I'll have Sebastian bring you here first thing in the morning."

"Promise?"

"Yes."

I turn to Harper and give her a hug. "I'm so glad you're okay."

"I'm like Cat Woman with nine lives." She winks at me. "Don't worry, I've still got five left."

Hayden and I say our goodbyes and he steers me from the room, to the elevators, and then into the waiting vehicle outside. Once I'm seated, I turn to face him.

"Thank you. I would've gone insane worrying about her."

"It was the right thing to do."

I smirk at him. "*After* you forced me to forgive you."

"If there's an opportunity to get what I want, I'm not going to ignore it."

"You really wanted my forgiveness that badly?"

He takes my hand, lacing his fingers through mine. "More than anything."

I lift a brow in question. "I thought you said you didn't care if I hated you?"

"The past few weeks showed me that I could lose you through hatred. I don't want that."

"You haven't lost me."

"Are you saying that I've won you?" He glares at me in warning. "If you say 'almost,' I will spank you until you change your mind."

I grin. "If you're willing to bring me to see my best friend, and all you asked was for me to forgive you? Then yes, you've won me."

He leans forward. "Say it again."

"You've won me, Hayden," I whisper against his mouth. "Now, what are you going to do with me?"

He smiles. "Keep you. That part of my plan has never changed."

CHAPTER 24

C alista

An hour later, I walk into Hayden's bedroom, freshly showered in a silk nightie. I locate him sitting on the bed, waiting for me. His eyes find mine, and I smile. It falters at the serious expression on his face.

"Everything okay?" When he nods, I tilt my head. "Then why are you looking at me like that?"

"I'm not used to seeing you with clothes on."

I shake my head with a smile. "You're going to have to get used to it. We're home now, so things have changed."

"Do you consider this your home, Callie?"

I bite my lip in thought. His gaze shifts to my mouth, his eyes darkening. Before I can answer his question, he holds out a hand and motions me forward. I walk up to him, and he takes my wrist, pulling me toward him until I'm standing between his legs.

"Yes," I whisper. "This is my home because you're here."

"You're my home." He lightly taps my chest, just above my heart. "This is where I want to be."

I cover his hand with mine, flattening it against my skin. "You are."

He nods, but retracts his hand and squeezes his eyes shut as though he's in pain. "Callie?" he says, his voice strained.

"What's wrong?"

"It's been *three* weeks."

"Three weeks since what?"

He looks up at me, the skin around his jaw tight. "I'm so fucking hard right now."

"*Oh.*"

He nods. I swallow thickly. His gaze moves to my throat and then lower. My nipples harden under his scrutiny.

"You need to leave," he grits out.

"Leave?" I frown. "Why?"

"Because if you stay, I'm going to fuck the shit out of you."

I blink down at him. "Okay."

"Don't lie to me. That's not what you want."

"How do you know?"

"Because fucking you is what *I* want, what *I* need."

"You think I don't need you too?"

He takes my chin and pulls me close enough for me to see the honesty in his eyes. "If you need me, then I'll give it to you. But only then."

"Hayden, I do need you. Maybe more than ever."

He nods and unbuttons his shirt, exposing his chest inch by inch. I watch him with anticipation as he reveals his sculpted abdomen, my hands itching to run my fingers over the firm ridges. Once he removes his clothes completely, he leans back and watches me.

"Come here, baby."

After removing my nightie, I step forward, and he pulls me onto his lap, my legs straddling him. Then he wraps an arm around me and yanks me even closer. I run my fingers through his hair, tugging it lightly as I bring my mouth to meet his.

He reaches up and palms my breasts, massaging them before pinching my nipples. I gasp and arch into him, enjoying his touch. His hands move lower, tracing every curve. He stops to run his thumb over my tattoo.

"You're so beautiful," he murmurs against my lips.

I grind onto his erection, my body humming with need. He's right. It has been too long. I want him so badly, I can hardly think.

Hayden breaks the kiss, his eyes blazing. "Now, say that you're mine."

"I'm yours."

"Again."

"I'm yours, Hayden. Completely."

With a low growl, he pulls us down onto the bed. Then he thrusts into me so hard that stars dance behind my eyelids, and I dig my nails into his shoulders, drawing blood.

"Fuck, Callie," he groans.

"Oh, God. Harder."

His body covers mine, and he drives into me again and again. I throw my head back and lean into the punishing rhythm. Then I grab his ass, pulling him to me, telling him I want more.

We're both close, and I know it won't take much for me to come. I cling to him as he pounds me into the mattress, continuing to fuck me. He uses one hand to grab my hip, digging his thumb into my tattoo as if to make sure it stays deep in my skin, marking me as his.

Then he grabs my throat, squeezing lightly, and I lose it. My orgasm explodes through me, making me scream out his name. And that I love him. His own release follows shortly after, and he collapses on top of me.

We lie there for a while, holding each other. The room is quiet except for the sounds of our heavy breathing. Eventually, Hayden rolls over and sits up on his forearm. He takes my chin and forces me to meet his gaze.

"Did you mean what you said?"

I grin. "'Oh, God. Harder?' I totally meant that."

He playfully swats my ass. "You know which part."

"Yes," I say, my tone serious. "And I did."

"Good."

"What about you?"

His eyes burn into me and he nods.

"Say it."

He traces my bottom lip with his thumb. "I didn't want to love you, Callie, but fuck me, I do. Possessively. Irrevocably. Completely."

I walk into Harper's room the next morning carrying two coffees with a huge smile on my face. Hayden loves me. I can't stop thinking about it.

"I brought coffee," I greet.

"Awesome. The shit they serve here doesn't have the right to be called coffee."

After placing her drink on the side table, I give her a quick hug and take the seat next to the bed. "You sound like you're in a good mood. Feeling better?"

"I'll be stuck here for another day, but that's not too bad."

"At least you'll be out of here before classes start."

She groans. "Ugh, don't remind me."

I laugh softly. "I'm sorry. I didn't think about your wrist."

She waves off my apology and takes a sip of coffee before setting the cup back down. "It's fine. I know you're excited to go back and you should be."

"I am. I finally feel like my life is coming together. I have you and Hayden, and now I'm continuing my education. I'm really happy."

"And yet you look exhausted."

I give her a wry grin. "I was up most of the night."

"I see." She waggles her brows at me. "How is the sex god today?"

"Fine. He told me he loved me."

"Get the fuck out? Wow. That's amazing."

"Thanks. I still can't believe it."

"It's nice that he's got the balls to admit what everyone else already knows. Did you say it back?"

I nod, my cheeks heating.

"Good. Now I'll just sit back and wait for the wedding."

"Harper, it's too early for that."

She wags her finger in my face. "You just wait. And when it happens, I'm going to be your maid of honor."

I shake my head with a smile. "You're ridiculous, but of course, you'll be my bridesmaid."

"Good morning, girls."

Harper and I turn to see a woman walk into the room. She's an older version of my best friend, except with her vibrant red hair cut in a short bob. Her green eyes are alert and hold a spark of intelligence that perfectly explains the pharmaceutical name badge attached to her pocket. Her navy pantsuit with a crisp white blouse and a pair of heels remind me of something Hayden bought for me. Something high-quality and stylish.

"Hey, mom," Harper says with a smile. "This is Calista. She's my friend from the Sugar Cube, remember?"

The woman nods. "Of course I do. It's nice to finally meet you. My daughter talks about you all the time. You can call me Melissa. Whenever someone calls me 'ma'am,' it makes me feel old."

"It's great to meet you as well," I say, taking her hand and shaking it. Her grip is firm, but her expression is welcoming. "Harper is lucky to have you."

Melissa's expression turns solemn as she retracts her arm. "I know this is late, but I'm so sorry for your loss. Your father was a very influential man, and we'll miss him."

"Thank you," I say, forcing the words past the lump in my throat. "This year has been very difficult, but things are turning around for me. I didn't realize you knew my father."

"Oh, yes. We worked with him on occasion."

"I'm sorry, but can you remind me of the company you work for?"

"AstraRx."

I school my features to hide my confusion. "Oh, right. I remember now."

The lie flows easily from my lips. I've been hanging out with Hayden too much. Having worked with my father's campaign manager, I should recognize the name. The fact that I don't isn't a big deal, but considering someone drugged me, that makes it one.

I glance at her badge again, noting the logo. Before I can say anything else, she turns away from me and takes Harper's hand in hers. "How are you feeling, honey? Better today?"

My best friend shrugs. "I'm bored out of my mind."

"You'll be out of here tomorrow."

I nod. "And you have me. I'll stay here until visiting hours end and they kick me out."

"That'll be great." Harper grins at me, her eyes crinkling at the corners. "It'll be even better if you've brought that bodyguard with you."

Melissa frowns. "Is that why there's a hulking bald man just outside the door? I was about to notify the hospital staff."

"My boyfriend is overprotective," I mumble.

"And hot." Harper grins at me. "If Mr. Bennett had a friend that was as good-looking as him, I'd be tempted to break the law."

I roll my eyes with a laugh and Melissa shakes her head. "It's hard to believe that I gave birth to you," she says to Harper. "But I have no regrets."

"Of course you don't. How long are you staying today, mom?"

The woman purses her lips. "Only until lunchtime. After that, I have to go into the office. We're rolling out a new drug and it's all hands on deck. If I'm not there, Mr. Russell gets testy."

Harper sits up in the bed and leans forward. "But you will be back tomorrow morning to pick me up, right? If I have to spend another full day here, I'm going to lose my shit."

"I'll be here first thing," Melissa says.

My friend visibly relaxes, flopping back on the pillow. "Good. Now I want to hear all about your vacation, Calista."

I inwardly cringe before launching into detail about the whole experience. Minus the part about how Hayden kidnapped me. And the naked part, too.

CHAPTER 25

C alista

"DON'T ARGUE WITH ME, SEBASTIAN."

I march over to the elevator of the penthouse and push the button. It lights up, and the doors immediately part. I step inside with my bodyguard on my heels, his face creased with concern as I select the first floor.

"Mrs. Bennett—"

When I shoot him a dirty look, he clears his throat. Just because I've accepted Hayden calling me that doesn't mean I'm ready for the rest of the world to do it too.

"Miss Calista, Mr. Bennett gave me strict instructions not to take you anywhere except the hospital to visit your friend. Now that she's been discharged, you're supposed to stay home."

"I understand your reasons for wanting to keep me safe. Not only is it your job, but Hayden is not someone who likes to be disobeyed. With that being said, you're not going to change my mind. I have to speak to Mr. Davis. *Today*."

Sebastian slams his hand on the door's edge, preventing it from closing. "I take my job seriously, so seriously, in fact, that I'll pick you up and carry you out of this elevator kicking and screaming if I have to."

I glare up at him in an effort to conceal my nervousness. "If you do, I'll tell Hayden that you groped me."

My stomach churns with acid at the lie. And the look of horror on Sebastian's face. He pales, and his eyes widen. If I wasn't trying to intimidate him, I'd be amused that this brawny man the size of a mountain is scared of Hayden.

"You wouldn't do that," he says.

"Wouldn't I?"

"Do you have any idea what that man would do to me if he thought I touched you?" The bodyguard shudders. "You're cruel to threaten me like this."

I quirk a brow. "Desperate times..."

He mutters something under his breath—a curse in Russian, if I were to guess—and folds his arms. "I'm doomed either way. If he doesn't kill me, I'll consider myself lucky."

"If he gives you a hard time about taking me out, then I'll advocate on your behalf."

He says something else in a foreign language, and when I frown at him, he says, "It's better to be at the right hand of the devil than to be in his path of destruction."

"Am I the devil?"

Sebastian sighs. "That depends on how Mr. Bennett reacts."

I take pity on the bodyguard and keep to myself, staying close to him as he guides me to and from the vehicle. The campaign headquarters hasn't changed one bit. I stop and stare at it briefly before Sebastian is ushering me indoors, his head on a constant swivel.

Once inside, I walk toward the offices at the rear of the building. Sure enough, Robert Davis sits at his desk, his eyes glued to the computer screen in front of him. I run my gaze over him, searching for any changes. His hair is still the same mousy brown, lying limply against his forehead, but his clothes are pressed and his tie straight.

For a moment, it's like I've been transported back in time when my father still lived and Mr. Davis was by his side for every event. My throat closes as emotion threatens to choke me. Sebastian briefly places a hand on my shoulder.

"Are you all right?"

"I will be. It's just that I haven't been here since my father died. I don't know why I didn't think it'd affect me to be here." I straighten my spine and nod. "Okay, I'm ready."

I walk up to the office door and grip the handle. Robert's head snaps in my direction as I open the door and step inside, with Sebastian right behind me. The manager blinks at me in confusion before rising from his chair with a smile.

"Miss Green, what a pleasure to see you again. I hope you've been well?"

"I have. Thank you, Robert."

He gazes at Sebastian and then returns his attention to me. "Is there something I can do for you?"

"Yes."

"Please have a seat." After Sebastian and I occupy the set of leather chairs in front of his desk, Robert sits as well. He clasps his hands and rests them on the desktop, leaning forward. "What can I help you with?"

"I want to know about my father's involvement with AstraRx."

Robert's eyes briefly flare before his gaze is shuttered.

"I'm sorry, Calista. I have no idea what you're talking about. Your father was a very busy man, but that's one company that he wasn't affiliated with."

"Please don't waste my time with lies. I spoke to Melissa Flynn yesterday, and she was very clear about working with my father in the past."

"Again, I regret to tell you that you're wrong. I don't know who this Flynn woman is, but she's obviously lying."

I take a deep breath in an attempt to calm my anger. "Given the fact that you're desperate to hide this from me tells me that whatever my father was involved in wasn't good. If you're trying to protect me or his memory, don't. I need the truth. My life might depend on it."

Robert squints at me. "Are you in some sort of trouble?"

Sebastian shifts his gaze from the manager to me. With the subtle movement, I sense what he's trying to say without words. "Okay, that might've been a little dramatic," I say, backtracking. "However, I want to know about my father's dealings. I need closure. It's been a year and I still don't have any answers concerning what happened to me *that night*."

"And you think AstraRx has something to do with the incident?" When I nod, he sighs. "Listen, Calista, I wish I could help you, but you're making connections that simply aren't there. Maybe it's best you forget this whole ordeal and put it behind you."

His words, condescending and judgmental, are like a match. Righteous indignation explodes within me.

I leap to my feet and snatch the letter opener off to my right. As soon as I curl my fingers around the gold-etched handle, I slam it into the desk, the tip disappearing into the wood right in front of him.

Robert jolts, and his eyes widen to the fullest extent. I can see myself in the darkness of his pupils, my chest heaving and my expression furious. Before he can react, I lean forward, still gripping the handle.

"I came here for answers, Robert. If you won't tell them to me, then you can deal with Sebastian here. He's more than a bodyguard, he's *Bratva*."

The manager throws up his arms, his palms facing me. "Okay, fine. Let's all calm down."

"Don't you know that telling a woman to 'calm down' has the opposite effect?" I narrow my gaze. "Start talking."

"Okay, fine. Yes, your father had dealings with AstraRx. More specifically, the owner, Thomas Russell."

With a firm jerk, I rip the letter opener from the wood with Robert watching my every move. After that I sink into my chair with the makeshift weapon resting on my lap. "For what?"

Robert scrubs his jaw with his hand, peering at me and then Sebastian. "Mr. Russell approached your father many years ago, at the beginning of his political career. The senator wasn't a fool, but he was much more impressionable back then. The owner of AstraRx ended up being a huge contributor to his very first campaign."

I clutch the handle until my hand shakes. "What did my father promise him in return?"

"At the time, the pharmaceutical company tried and failed to launch a new drug that had the potential to make millions of dollars. It kept getting flagged by the FDA because of detrimental side effects. Your father voted on certain laws that allowed AstraRx to bypass some of the red tape and ease the distribution of the drug into the market."

"Oh, my God." I slump in my chair and bow my head. "Are you saying that my father knowingly helped put a dangerous drug into the hands of the public in exchange for funding?"

"I'm so sorry, Calista."

"Why would he do that?" I whisper. "My father was a good man. He'd never willingly hurt anyone."

Robert shakes his head slowly, either in disagreement or in pity. "Everyone has skeletons in their closet. It's only a matter of when they're exposed."

I sit motionless as his words sink in. My father, the honorable senator I've idolized all my life, helped unscrupulously distribute a dangerous drug just to further his political ambitions. How did I not see this part of him?

"He was a different man back then, Calista," Robert says gently. "I think once he got entangled with that company, it was hard to extricate himself. But he eventually did. We all make mistakes, especially when we let moments of weakness rule us."

I shake my head, sorrow mixing with anger inside me. "A mistake is accidentally running a red light, not sacrificing public health for power and greed."

"What's done is done," Robert says. "Your father came to deeply regret those early unethical choices. He spent the later part of his career fighting hard for consumer protection laws."

"That doesn't make it right. Who knows how many lives were ruined or lost because of his actions?" I pause. "When did my father finally stop dealing with AstraRx?"

Robert drums his fingers on the desk. When he finally answers me, there's a veil of guilt covering his face. "I think it was approximately a year ago."

I close my eyes, suddenly exhausted. My image of the principled, heroic father I loved has been shattered. The letter opener slips from my fingers and clatters to the floor.

"Are you ready to leave, Miss Green?" Sebastian asks, keeping his gaze on Robert.

As if the manager could hurt me any more than he has already.

I take a shaky breath. "Yes." I look at Robert. "Thank you for telling me the truth, even though it was hard to hear."

"I know I haven't been around much since the funeral, but if you need anything, don't hesitate to call." Robert gets to his feet, and I follow suit. He reaches for me and immediately drops his hands at Sebastian's glare. "Senator Green may not have been the most ethical politician, but he was a wonderful father before his untimely death."

A thought strikes the heart of me, making my pulse race and my skin sweat. What if this pharmaceutical company was involved with my father's murder?

I bend down to retrieve the letter opener. Once I'm upright, I lift my chin and pin Robert with a hard look. "I'm going to keep looking into my father's death until I find who's responsible. If you had anything to do with it, tell me now."

Robert raises his hands. "No, Calista. I swear it. The only thing I'm guilty of is not talking your father out of that mess."

I pocket the letter opener inside my coat, not only as a keepsake but to issue a warning. "I hope you're telling the truth."

Sebastian follows me as I hurry out of the office building with the letter opener heavy in my pocket. The morning air hits my face, unsuccessfully cooling the turbulent emotions burning inside me. I stop on the sidewalk, wrapping my arms around myself as I try to steady my breathing to keep from having a panic attack.

My bodyguard approaches me while maintaining a respectful distance. "I know this is a lot to take in," he says.

"But you're not alone in this. Although I'm certain Mr. Bennett won't like seeing you upset, he does care for you."

I nod, not trusting my voice yet. A few rebellious tears slip down my cheeks.

Sebastian offers me a handkerchief from his pocket. I take it with a whispered "Thank you" and then dab my eyes.

"Whatever mistakes your father made, he clearly regretted them and tried to make amends," Sebastian continues. "You admired him for good reason. That hasn't changed."

I shake my head. "I feel like I didn't really know him. I'm not sure how to reconcile the scheming politician with the man who put Band-Aids on my scratches as a kid."

"Sometimes people have more than one side to them. The one they show the world and the one they keep hidden. That doesn't mean you can't love part of them."

"I don't know how to love in pieces. When I give someone my heart, I share all of it."

"Mr. Bennett is a very fortunate man then."

I sigh, folding the handkerchief neatly before offering it to Sebastian. "Maybe you don't want this back?"

"You keep it, Miss Green. Hopefully, you won't need it again anytime soon."

CHAPTER 26

C alista

"Please take me to Hayden's office."

Sebastian turns around in the driver's seat. His expression is conflicted, but at the fresh tears streaming down my cheeks, he nods slowly. "Okay, Miss Calista. But first, you have to give me your word on two things."

I bite my lip. "What are they?"

"First off, you have to tell Mr. Bennett this was your idea and that I had nothing to do with it. Also, add in that I tried to talk you out of it."

Sebastian's potent unease when it comes to Hayden still amuses me, but I keep my face blank, not wanting to embarrass him. "I promise. What's the second thing?"

"I don't want you to cry anymore." The giant man blows out a breath and rubs the back of his neck. "I've never been good at handling a woman's tears. It's hard for me to see you upset."

My heart melts. "I'll do my best."

"Thank you."

He turns back around and shifts the car into drive before pulling out onto the street. I remove the letter opener from my pocket and run my fingernail over the engraving on the blade. This was a gift from my father to Robert, thanking him for his hard work during the first campaign. I wonder if he kept it because it's a useful tool, or if Robert still has it because it reminds him of my father and the friendship they shared.

I fiddle with the item until the vehicle comes to a stop. After putting it in my coat pocket, I open the car door and step outside. Sebastian is there with a frown of disapproval on his face.

"How many times do I have to tell you that I'll get the door for you?"

"I might've grown up as a senator's daughter, but I'm perfectly capable of opening a car door."

Sebastian scans the area—like he's been doing since we parked—his gaze briefly settling on mine. "It's a sign of respect, Miss Calista."

I reach out and pat his arm. "I appreciate that."

His frown deepens, and the skin of his neck flushes with color. After clearing his throat, he says, "Let's get you inside. Every second you're not indoors makes you susceptible to danger."

He motions for me to walk, and I take off at a rapid pace, not wanting to linger. It's not as though I've forgotten my situation, but sometimes I block it from my mind in favor of a peaceful existence. One that's recently been decimated by my father's past dealings.

Once inside, I walk up to Josephine. The moment she sees me, the woman sits up in her chair and adjusts her glasses. "Good morning, Mrs. Bennett. Are you here to see your husband today?"

I paste a smile on my face, pointedly ignoring the chuckle coming from Sebastian. At least the man has the decency to smother his laughter with a cough. Looking at the secretary, I nod.

"Is Hayden available?"

"Even if he wasn't, he gave me strict instructions to interrupt him, no matter what he's doing." She winks at me. "My boss doesn't have any restrictions when it comes to you."

You have no idea. "Thank you."

"Would you like me to escort you?" The hopeful gleam in her eyes has me shaking my head. "Very well," she says. "Enjoy the rest of your day, Mrs. Bennett."

After giving her a small wave, I spin on my heel and head toward Hayden's office. Sebastian is by my side in an instant, his long stride easily overtaking my small one.

"So, Mrs. Bennett..."

I glare up at him, but it lacks heat. "Don't start with me."

"Callie."

At the sound of Hayden's voice, both Sebastian and I jerk our heads in his direction. The attorney stands just outside his office, looking so gorgeous that any annoyance I had toward Sebastian fades.

Hayden holds out a hand, and my steps quicken. "What are you doing here? Is everything all right?" He snaps his gaze to Sebastian, the inquiry directed at him.

"She wanted to see you, sir. I couldn't talk her out of it, no matter how much I argued with her."

Hayden's gaze softens the instant it lands on me. I refrain from throwing myself into his embrace. Instead, I take his offered hand, taking comfort in the strength of his grip.

With his free hand, Hayden clasps the side of my neck,

gently pulling me in for a kiss. It's quick but passionate, causing me to stare up at him in a daze, my lips tingling.

"Sebastian's right," I say, my voice breathless. "I wouldn't listen to him."

Hayden's gaze darts to the other man. "Wait outside."

My bodyguard gives his employer a curt nod. I follow Hayden into his office, and once we're inside with the door shut and locked, I open my mouth to tell him all about my father.

I don't get the chance.

Hayden is on me in the blink of an eye. He slams his mouth to mine and spears my lips with his tongue, dominating my senses. I sag in his embrace, clutching the material of his dress shirt to keep from plummeting to the floor. When he finally breaks the kiss, my breaths are short little pants, and my chest heaves with every inhalation.

"Not that I mind, but what was that greeting for?" I ask.

"I needed it. One taste wasn't enough. Now why are you here, disobeying my orders as usual?"

I drop my gaze as shame washes over me. "I learned something about my father today. It gutted me, Hayden. I had to see you because I'm falling apart."

Hayden leads me over to the chair behind his desk and sits, pulling me onto his lap. He wraps his arms around me, resting his chin on the top of my head after placing a kiss on my temple.

"Tell me everything," he whispers.

So I do. By the time I'm done, I'm crying again. I retrieve the handkerchief that Sebastian gave me, already damp with my tears from earlier, and wipe my face.

"The man I idolized is a stranger to me," I say. "It's like I've lost him all over again. Now I have to bury the idea of him, the one I grew up loving."

"I understand. Although I cared for my mother, it was difficult reconciling her with the woman who was a drug addict. People are complicated."

"I know." I sigh and grip the handkerchief tighter. "But that doesn't make this any less painful for me to swallow."

Hayden goes silent for a moment, but when he speaks again, his body tenses against mine. "Did you find out the name of the pharmaceutical company he was in bed with?"

"Oh, right. AstraRx. It's owned by Thomas Russell, who was my father's point of contact. You know, it's crazy, but that's the same company Harper's mother works for."

"She does?" he asks, his voice deceptively soft.

"Yes. When I visited Harper in the hospital, her mother stopped by as well. That's where I saw her work badge." I reach out and take a notepad and pen, drawing the symbol from memory. "This is the logo. Do you know it?"

If I thought Hayden was stiff before, now he's like stone. "Are you certain that's the company's logo?"

"Yes, why? Do you know them?" I swallow as a thought surfaces. "You don't think Harper's mom was another one of my father's contacts, do you?"

"I don't know, but I'm going to find out."

I lean back so I can see his face. "Please don't do anything crazy. Harper would never forgive me if something happened to her mother. Promise me, Hayden."

He clenches his jaw, his gaze churning with his thoughts. And his rage. "I promise I won't hurt her. That's the best I can do."

"That's not very reassuring," I mumble. At a normal volume, I say, "Better than nothing. Thank you." I throw my arms around his neck and give him a quick kiss. "Hopefully, this new information will lead us to whoever sent me that box, and possibly identify my father's killer. Mr. Davis, my father's campaign manager, said that my father did everything he could to make things right. If he refused to work with AstraRx, then maybe that's what led to his murder. I have to believe that he was a good man when he died, or nothing in my life will make sense."

"Shhh. Don't worry about your father. What's most important is you and keeping you safe."

"But if they killed my father because of his involvement, then why are they coming after me? I had nothing to do with any of that. It's not like I knew before today."

"I don't have an answer for you. Regardless, you need to go home and stay there."

I sigh. "Fine. What time will you be off work?"

"Same as usual."

"Okay."

Hayden assists me to my feet and leads me to the door. After opening it, he looks at Sebastian. "Take Callie home."

"Yes, sir." The bodyguard looks at me. "Right this way, Mrs. Bennett."

I make a face at Hayden. He winks at me. I can't help but smile before allowing Sebastian to escort me through the building. Once I'm settled in the backseat, I go limp, letting my head fall back against the plush seating. Telling Hayden about my father's unscrupulous actions was difficult. Not that Hayden has any room to talk after stalking me, but I didn't want to taint his view of the man who raised me. I can't stand the idea of Hayden seeing me in the same light.

Thankfully, Sebastian maintains his professional demeanor on the way home, leaving us to sit in silence. Although I do catch his eyes darting to me in the rearview mirror on occasion. I smile at him once to reassure him that I'm fine before staring blankly out the window. The day's revelations have left me emotionally drained, and for once, I'm ready to listen to Hayden and stay home to recoup.

The vehicle slows to a stop at a red light when a flash of color catches my eye. It's a magenta jacket, bright and familiar. The tiny owner of the coat races down the sidewalk.

Completely alone.

CHAPTER 27

C alista

I sit straight up, catching Sebastian's attention. "What's wrong, Miss Calista?"

"I know her," I say, pointing to the child. "Where's her mother? She'd never leave Erika alone."

Before Sebastian can react, I throw open the door and sprint across the street. Erika rounds a corner and disappears from sight. My heart lurches in my chest.

I pump my arms at my sides and increase my speed, fueled by adrenaline and fear. As I turn down the alley and skid to a halt. Erika stands fifteen feet from me, her eyes wide with terror. A man dressed entirely in black has one hand clamped over the child's mouth while the other holds a gun to her head.

"Come with me, or she's dead," he says, his voice muffled behind the ski mask.

I slowly raise my hands. "Please don't hurt her. If you let her go, I'll do anything you want."

"Get your ass over here," the man says.

"Everything is going to be okay, Erika. Just stay calm."

She nods at me. Tears spill down the girl's cheeks, making my heart twist inside my chest. Once I'm standing next to the stranger, he pushes the child away, forcing her to the pavement. He grabs my upper arm and digs the muzzle of the pistol into my side.

"Move."

"Okay," I say quietly, putting on a calm facade for Erika. She watches me from the concrete as she slowly gets to her feet. "Don't worry about me."

"I'm sorry, Miss Calista." She sniffs. "He told me my mommy was here."

"It's going to be all right. I'm sure she's looking for you. Find a police officer to help you, all right?"

I watch her hesitate before she bolts. The man takes a step, pulling me along while keeping his firearm pressed against my rib cage. My heart thumps so loudly it drowns out the sounds of the city around us and I can't do anything except focus on that, willing the organ to not give out.

Until I hear my name.

Sebastian shouts my name for a second time and appears at the entrance of the alleyway like an avenging angel, his weapon drawn. The expression of ire on his face shifts into something ferocious when it lands on the man holding me captive.

"Let her go," he says, the demand echoing in the tight space between the buildings.

The stranger scoffs. "Fuck off." The man shoves me to the side and takes up a stance behind me, with the muzzle now digging into my spine. When Sebastian doesn't react, the man raises his voice. "I said, back the fuck off. If you don't, I'll kill her."

Sebastian shakes his head. "No, you won't. Someone paid you to take her alive. If not, you'd already have shot her."

"You're right," the man says.

My captive adjusts the firearm from my back to the space between my arm and body. I scream when the gun goes off. Sebastian shouts in pain and throws himself behind a dumpster lining the brick wall. But not before I catch the blood spreading across his abdomen.

As soon as my bodyguard disappears from sight, the shooter yanks me backward, leading me deeper into the alley. I struggle against his hold, yelling and kicking until he slaps me on the side of the head with his pistol.

Stars light up my vision, blurring everything in front of me. I close my eyes and concentrate on not throwing up from the onslaught of pain. My captor grips me just underneath my armpits and drags me.

My inner fortitude screams at me to fight. Once I'm taken away, my chances of survival decrease drastically. With a burst of desperation, I lean down and bite the man's wrist. He grunts in pain, loosening his grip. I plant my feet and wrench free, every part of me focused on escape.

He tackles me to the ground, and my head hits the pavement with a sickening crunch. The pain that explodes in my head is enough to debilitate me to the point that I don't move when he picks me up and tosses me over his shoulder. Only when he deposits me in the vehicle do I finally succumb to the darkness looming over me.

My last thought before I pass out is of Hayden.

"I didn't want to love you, Callie, but fuck me, I do. Possessively. Irrevocably. Completely."

~

I WAKE SLOWLY, BOTH MY HEAD AND HEART POUNDING.

For different reasons.

When I try to move, I can't. Not because I'm bound, but due to the fact that I'm groggy.

No, it's more than that. I compare this feeling to the lethargy I felt on the night of my assault, and my breaths quicken. Or struggle to.

I've been drugged.

I crack open my eyelids a sliver and take in my surroundings as my vision comes into focus, albeit still hazy. The living room is sparsely furnished with a faded green couch and a coffee table that has more scratches than the veneer covering the surface. The wallpaper is peeling in some places, and the color scheme is severely outdated, but the man standing a few feet away is impeccably dressed. The designer suit doesn't belong in this decrepit house, but then again, neither do I.

"Awake at last, Miss Green," he says, his voice smooth. It drips over me like oil, staining me where I'm lying on the threadbare carpet. "You slept for a long time. So long, in fact, I began to worry."

I open my mouth to speak, but I only manage a pained croak. He frowns and tilts his head, studying me. "Hmm. I'm not ready for you to overdose just yet."

Fear coils within me, combining with the disgust roiling in my gut. Knowing I'm at this monster's mercy is one thing, but knowing he's definitely going to kill me is another.

He snaps his fingers, startling me. A henchman, the one who kidnapped me, appears with a glass of water. The man in the suit takes it and walks over to me, crouching down. He holds the rim to my lips, and I drink. The chemical taste in my mouth remains, and my body is still sluggish, but at least I'm a little more coherent.

He sets the glass on the coffee table and braces his fore-arms on the tops of his thighs. He smiles at me, the cruelty gleaming in his brown eyes. "Looks like putting that redhead in the hospital was enough to draw you out. I was having a hell of a time finding you and Mr. Bennett."

"What?"

He continues as if I hadn't spoken. "You are very pretty. Too pretty, in fact. I haven't forgotten you, you know."

Even though everything inside me wants to hide, I force myself to meet his gaze head-on. I won't show him how intimidated I am, no matter what he has planned for me. If I'm going to die, it'll be with my pride intact.

"I assume you don't remember me, or you would've contacted me by now, Calista."

I can't stop the shudder that streaks through my body. The way he says my name is with a familiarity that's disturb-ing. My tongue is heavy in my mouth, but I force myself to speak, my need for answers bubbling up in my throat.

"What...what do you want?" I manage to rasp out. "Who are you?"

"I saw you once at a political party when you were very young." The man's smile widens, taking on a malicious edge. "I knew your father very well."

"Thomas Russell."

He nods. "Guilty. Once Mr. Bennett arrives, all of your questions will be answered."

"Hayden? What does he have to do with this?"

"He has *everything* to do with this."

CHAPTER 28

H ayden

THE MINUTE CALISTA LEAVES MY LINE OF SIGHT, I HEAD BACK
into my office and shut the door. Then proceed to mutter
every foul word I can think of until I'm less likely to kill
someone before my workday ends. I think.

The jury's still out on that.

I throw myself into my chair and the leather emits a
squeak of protest. "Fucking AstraRx. How did I not make
the connection?"

After retrieving the pill from my drawer, I lay it next to
the drawing Calista left behind, looking at them with fresh
eyes. The symbol from the pharmaceutical company isn't
the same as the one on the drug, but the starburst is hidden
within it. I caught that as Calista was drawing it. The first
couple of strokes of the pen revealed the shape before it was
covered with the modern logo.

"Your balls must be huge if you didn't bother to get rid of

that symbol completely," I say. "It could've, and did, leave a trail straight to you."

After pulling my laptop closer, I type the company's name into the search and hit enter. The information before me is nothing out of the ordinary, but it's not as though I expected to find signs pointing to illegal activities on their front page.

This website has everything that's expected. And legal. I click on the directory, and Melissa Flynn's profile stares back at me. The similarities between the woman and her daughter are uncanny.

"Are you involved?" I mutter to myself. "Did you know what Senator Green was doing? Or was Thomas Russell his only point of contact?"

After selecting the link to the owner of AstraRx, I study the man, taking in his blond hair and brown eyes. At first glance, he appears to be the standard ambitious businessman, complete with an expensive suit and a shrewd gaze. The only thing that catches my attention is his age and the number of years he's owned this corporation.

He's old enough to be responsible for manufacturing the drug that led to my mother's death...

The thought hits me, stealing the breath from my lungs. I suck in ragged gulps of air while my chest heaves until my heartbeats stop clanging in my head.

"I'm coming for you, motherfucker." I tap the screen, distorting the pixels. "Going after my mother is one thing, but targeting Calista?" I shake my head. "I'm going to enjoy peeling your skin from your body."

I sit there and lose track of time going through every drug AstraRx put on the market. When my cell phone chimes with an incoming call, I rub my eyes before picking it up and looking at the screen. An unknown number flashes and the hairs on the nape of my neck straighten.

"Who's this?" I answer, my voice harsh.

"Hello." The man on the line sounds cheerful, a saccharine tone that instantly grates on my nerves. "Mr. Bennett, I have something that belongs to you."

A low moan in the background, followed by a feminine grunt of pain, has my hands shaking. With both rage and fear.

No. God, no.

"Miss Green sends her love," the man says. "Although not for much longer."

I grip the edge of my desk to keep from punching it. Whoever the fuck this is can't know how rattled I am by Calista's condition. He can't know that I'm about to drop to my knees in agony at the idea of her being hurt.

"Where is she?" I ask, concentrating on keeping my words even. "I want to talk to her."

"One second."

A cry of pain hits my ears, and I can feel the blood draining from my face.

Fuck.

FUCK!

How did this happen? I just saw Calista less than an hour ago.

The man chuckles. "You're not in any position to be demanding anything, Mr. Bennett."

"What do you want?"

"You have one hour to show up at the address that's being sent to you right now. Otherwise, Miss Green's body will be delivered to your address. In pieces."

The call disconnects, leaving me to stare at my phone in stunned disbelief.

"No..."

My stomach drops.

This can't be fucking happening.

Not to her.

I immediately call Sebastian, ready to rip his arms from his body if he doesn't answer. After several agonizing seconds, I finally hang up. The fact that he didn't take my call is all I need to know. Hopefully, he's not dead. I'm quick to shoot off a message to Zack to have someone look into his disappearance.

The address the mysterious man spoke of comes through on a text, as well as a warning to come alone and unarmed. I read it with a frown, my brows pulling together. It's in an industrial part of the city. A place I used to be familiar with. Why would he take Calista there?

It doesn't matter. I just need to get to her.

I plant my feet and stand, shoving my chair back so forcefully it slams into the wall. Then I'm through the door and striding toward the elevator that leads to the underground parking garage.

"Mr. Bennett, I was going to ask if you'd like your usual lunch, but you seem in a hurry," Josephine calls out from behind her desk.

"Cancel it, Josephine. I'll be back later."

"But, sir—"

I don't let her finish as I rush toward the set of metal doors. "Come on!" I growl, pressing the button repeatedly. Finally, they part, and I step inside, tapping my foot as the damn elevator moves at a slow pace.

When the doors open, I step out onto the garage level. My driver is already standing by the open door of my vehicle, waiting to assist me, and I wave him off.

"I'll be driving today."

I PULL UP TO MY CHILDHOOD HOME.

This motherfucker brought Calista here to torment me. There's no other explanation for this specific choice in location.

I grip the steering wheel so tightly, my knuckles turn white, and a tingling sensation skitters along my fingers. The longer I stare at the house, the more nauseous I become. I promised myself that I'd never step foot in this godforsaken place again.

This is where my mother died.

But I'll be damned if the same thing happens to Calista.

Taking a deep breath, I get out of the car and stride up the walkway. When I reach the front door, I'm tempted to pound on it with my fist. Instead, I rap my knuckles against it once. No need to do more than that when the asshole inside is expecting me.

The door opens, and the same man whose face was just displayed on my computer screen stands in the foyer. Thomas Russell holds a firearm, the barrel pointed at my chest.

"So glad you could make it, Mr. Bennett," he says, his eyes dark and sinister. "You arrived faster than I guessed you would. Looks like Miss Green means more to you than I thought."

"Where is she?"

"Why don't you come inside and make yourself at home?" Russell chuckles. "Considering you used to live here, I think that was quite clever of me. Pun intended."

The sound of his amusement has me shaking with the need to hit him, but my need to see Calista overrules it. I stride forward and come to an abrupt halt when I find her lying on the floor. Completely motionless.

My heart drops, and I race to her side, kneeling to take her pulse. It's weak but there. Relief swamps me while I battle the urge to pull her into my arms. My instincts scream at me in protest when I retract my hands, but I can't show weakness.

Calista looks so fragile, her skin pale and her breathing labored. She blinks slowly, and I can tell the minute she recognizes me because she mouths my name. It guts me. I thought I knew heartache, but I didn't really until this moment.

I rise, turn to Russell, and glare at him, not bothering to hide my fury. "What did you give her?"

"Oh, nothing that would kill her right away," he says, leaning against the wall with his arms crossed. "You and I need to have a little chat first."

I look around, and a flashback from my youth surfaces.

I'm a child, coming home after school to find my mom collapsed on the living room floor right where Calista lies. My mother's skin had that same sickly pallor, her breaths shallow and pained. The fear in that moment caused me to panic. I stared at her for several minutes with the certainty that I was losing her. Then I pleaded with her to wake up before the ambulance arrived and proclaimed her deceased.

Now, seeing Calista like this...It terrifies me. I've never been more scared in my entire life.

"I'm going to kill you," I say quietly.

"Yeah, like you did Senator Green?"

Fuck.

I freeze, cold dread washing over me at his words. He *knows*. Somehow, this vile man knows the truth about what happened between me and Calista's father.

"Oh come now, don't play dumb," he says. "I know all about your little confrontation with the dear senator that night."

Calista stirs by my side, inhaling sharply, but I can't look at her. I don't want to see the look of hurt on her face. And I don't want her to see the look of guilt sure to be on mine.

CHAPTER 29

C alista

"I'M GOING TO KILL YOU," HAYDEN SAYS TO MY CAPTOR.

"Yeah, like you did Senator Green?"

I stare up at Hayden, waiting for him to deny it. He doesn't look at me. Anxiety slams into me, and my heart stutters in my chest. Why isn't he saying anything?

"Oh come now, don't play dumb." Russell shakes his head, clicking his tongue in admonishment. "I know all about your little confrontation with the dear senator that night."

For the first time, I think death might not be the worst thing to happen to me. As if I've been kicked in the stomach, I suck in a breath and curl in on myself. Part of me wants to reach out and grasp Hayden's leg to anchor myself emotionally, while the rest recoils at the idea.

"Whatever it is that you think you know is wrong," Hayden says.

Russell holds his arms out. "How can I be wrong when I'm the one that put you up to it?"

Hayden doesn't move, but the muscles in his legs tense underneath his slacks. If they weren't in my line of sight, I doubt I would've been able to tell. I glance up at him again and then Russell, unsure of who I should watch. Which man is my true enemy?

Right now, they both are.

"What are you talking about?" Hayden asks.

"You think you're the only person who employs a hacker?" Russell lets his arms fall to his sides with a slap. "I made sure to plant 'clues' that would lead you to believe the senator killed his secretary. It was actually me, by the way."

"Why?" I say, my voice barely above a wheeze.

Both men glance in my direction, but I keep my focus on Russell. My desperation for knowledge overrides everything.

"Your father helped me a lot when I first bought AstraRx," Russell says, holding my stare. "When I wrote my doctoral thesis, it was about depressants and their effects on the central nervous system. After buying the pharmaceutical company, I wanted to expand that research and develop a marketable drug. Unfortunately, I couldn't get it to pass FDA standards until Senator Green got involved. But that didn't stop me from putting it out on the street."

He turns to Hayden. "Your addict mother came into contact with it through her boyfriend and died in this very room. It might comfort you to know she wasn't the only person who overdosed. That drug was so potent, it didn't take much to cross the line."

"You son of a bitch!" Hayden takes a step forward, and I throw out my arm to grab his shoe. He stills at the contact and drops his gaze to me. When our eyes meet, I swallow at the unholy rage burning in their depths.

"Don't," I whisper.

"Listen to her." Russell nods in my direction. "If you don't, you'll get yourself killed faster than I'd like. Anyway, after that debacle with the first drug, I moved on to something else. The users call it a roofie, but it has the potency of Valium. It creates the effect of cocaine binge while feeling the high similar to being on heroin."

He sighs. "It's a thing of beauty. Don't you agree, Calista? After all, this is your second time experiencing the narcotic. I doubt you remember the first time I gave it to you in the children's center."

"Oh, my God." My stomach heaves as memories, both clear and muddled, barrage my mind. I gag until I'm sick all over the carpet. "It was you."

Hayden gently lifts me onto the dusty couch before spinning to face Russell. "Did you rape her?"

I watch the exchange while struggling to control my panicked breathing. The letter opener digs into my side and I slowly dip my hand inside my coat, concentrating on keeping my expression dazed. If the man who kidnapped me had searched me like he did Hayden, he would've removed the only weapon available to me.

"I'm sure you'd like to know what I did to her while she was passed out." The man lifts a sardonic brow. "But as much as I'd love to continue fucking with your mind, I really want to get to the reason why I brought you both here. Mr. Bennett, did you really think you could kill all of those people and get away with it?" Russells asks with an incredulous expression. "I've been watching you for many years. It might've taken me a while to pin certain deaths on you, but eventually, I figured out the pattern. If you

189

hadn't researched my company on the government databases once you became an attorney, I might've never found you."

Hayden folds his arms. "Really?"

"You only kill someone who you can't put behind bars through the legal system," Russell says, his attention on Hayden. "Matthews. Parkinson. Deter. You're an intelligent man. Don't tell me you don't recognize the names of your victims."

"I'd be lying if I said they weren't familiar to me."

"Familiar? Ha!" Russell slaps his thigh. "You got pretty familiar when you slit their throats and buried their bodies. Attorneys, always carefully choosing what they will and won't admit to."

I wrap my trembling fingers around the handle. I might end up shot before I have a chance to use it, but I have to try. Hayden tilts head and simply waits. He bristles with something more explosive that rage and more violent that hatred.

I don't know how much longer he can contain that dark energy. I have to be ready.

"Do you know how hard it is to find criminals that are intelligent enough to not get caught, but if they do, they don't take you down with them?" Russell sighs. "Take my word for it. It's very challenging. To make matters worse, there's a certain *prosecutor* who's very good at putting my drug dealers out of business by sending them to prison or sending them to hell after he kills them."

"The justice system isn't always just," Hayden says with a nonchalant shrug. "How was I supposed to know that you were putting drugs on the streets to be distributed for your own gain? If I would've known, I could've killed you instead and saved myself a lot of trouble."

Russell takes a menacing step toward Hayden but stops

when he narrows his gaze. "I've lost millions because of you, you arrogant prick!"

"That's nothing I haven't been called before. You're going to need to be better than that if you want to upset me."

"Is this enough for you?" He aims the gun at me. "You talk a lot, Bennett, but don't forget who has all the power."

Hayden holds up his hands in a show of surrender. "Easy, Russell."

"Now you want to placate me?" The man's lip curls with a sneer. "Go fuck yourself."

He walks over to where I'm lying on the couch, keeping the firearm pointed down at me. "Back up!" As soon as Hayden does, Russell snatches up a handful of my hair and presses the muzzle against my temple. "I'm going to enjoy watching you suffer when she dies."

I don't hesitate. I jab the letter opener into his thigh with all the strength I can summon. Russell lets out a howl of pain right before Hayden lunges, tackling him to the ground. The gun lands on the floor with a thud.

My vision tilts when I climb from the couch and onto the carpet on my hands and knees. I push myself into motion, despite the drugs in my system slowing me down. All I can think about is getting the weapon.

Hayden lands a punch to Russell's jaw, and the man's head snaps back. When I'm less than a foot away from the firearm, Hayden snatches it up. He swings the barrel toward the front door and pulls the trigger as the door opens to reveal the henchman.

I cry out at the loud noise, but don't move. I stare transfixed as red blooms on the man's chest before he plummets to the ground. Hayden steals my attention when he gets to his feet.

With my pulse thumping in my ears, I watch him as he

grabs a pillow from the couch and presses the gun's muzzle against it. My mouth falls open at the makeshift silencer.

Then he shoots Russell. Twice. One bullet in each kneecap.

Hayden stands over him with a satisfied smile while the man sobs in pain. "That'll keep you from running while I get Calista to a hospital, but when I get back, you and I are going to have a little chat."

My head spins. Not only from the drugs, but from the effort to process everything that I just learned.

Hayden murdered my father. Not just him, but countless others.

Russell killed my father's secretary and assaulted me to intimidate my father and keep him in line. And now Hayden will kill him for that and for indirectly murdering his mother.

I'm not going to be sane ever again.

Hayden tucks the gun into his waistband and crouches down next to me. I look up at him, not bothering to hide my accusatory expression. "How could you?" I ask, tears stinging my eyes.

He doesn't answer me. Instead, Hayden gathers me into his arms and holds me close to his chest. His heart pounds furiously against my ear, and his grip on me is tighter than normal.

"Let's get you to a hospital, Callie. I'll explain everything later. I promise."

His voice is gentle, but I can detect the concern underneath. He cares for me. I don't doubt that, yet how can I believe anything he says?

CHAPTER 30

C alista

My eyes flutter open to harsh fluorescent lights. The familiar, steady beeping of a nearby machine fills my ears, and the hint of antiseptic hits my nose. I'm in a hospital.

A-fucking-gain.

I immediately search for Hayden, both relieved and disappointed by his absence. The last time I was here, he never left my side. Flashes of memory return—Russell, the secrets, the gunshots.

A sickening feeling roils in my gut. If Hayden's not here, he's with Russell, making good on his promise to avenge his mother. And me.

I can't deny the sick satisfaction of knowing my attacker is dead. Or about to be, if anything he said about Hayden was true. I believe it is, or I wouldn't be nervous at the idea of seeing him.

A nurse enters the room, her rubber soles squeaking on

the tiled floor. "Oh, good, you're awake," she says with a bright smile. "We were starting to get worried when you didn't wake up right away after having your stomach pumped."

I place a hand on my abdomen, my throat too dry for me to respond. As if sensing my discomfort, the nurse hands me a cup of water. After a few sips, I try again. "What happened to me?"

Although I know the answer, I'm cautious since I have no idea what Hayden told the hospital staff when he brought me here. I may not trust him, but I'm too upset to make any decisions that could land him in prison.

"You had quite an ordeal, but you're safe now," the woman says.

I flick my gaze to her name tag. "Thank you, Nicole."

"Absolutely. Thank goodness you threw up most of the pills. Otherwise..." She trails off and grimaces. "Anyway, there's no need to worry."

I shudder, recalling the moment Russell held me at gunpoint and told me to swallow the pills. "Good. Where's Mr. Bennett, the man who brought me here?"

"Your husband was here until the procedure was finished and you were stable. He told me to tell you that he'd be back and not to panic."

A hysterical bit of laughter rises in my throat, and I swallow it down. His lack of presence wouldn't send me into panic mode. It's the complete opposite at this point. I school my features with a look of consternation.

"Oh, I can't believe I forgot to tell you," she says. "The baby is going to be just fine. It hasn't suffered any effects from the drugs, which is a blessing."

I blink at her. "Pregnant? That can't be right. Are you

sure you got all of the drugs out of my system? I just imagined you said something that's impossible."

The woman grins at me. "It's *definitely* possible."

"No, I'm on the shot." I shake my head emphatically. "I got it weeks ago."

Her smile disappears. She grabs the chart from the side table, confusion clouding her face. "No, it says right here that you're approximately four weeks pregnant."

I don't need a mirror to confirm the look of horror on my face. The nurse gives me a sympathetic pat on the arm. "The shot is about 94% effective, and no birth control is 100%," she says. "You may have fallen into that small percentage where it failed."

"Did you tell Hayden? I mean, my husband?" When she shakes her head, I go limp against the mattress. "Okay, please don't. I want to be the one to do it."

She nods. "Don't forget about HIPAA. Don't designate him to have access to your medical files if you don't want him to know."

"Thank you. I'll be sure to remember that."

The idea of Hayden knowing I'm pregnant is enough to make me faint. After everything that's happened between us, he deserves the chance to explain Russell's accusations. But my intuition knows something I can't seem to wrap my mind around.

He's guilty.

I STARE AT THE CEILING, STILL REELING FROM THE NEWS THAT I'M pregnant.

What am I going to do?

This baby has a mother who's not completely without funds, but she doesn't exactly have a career in place to provide a comfortable life. On the other hand, the father has more than enough money, but he's a murderer.

Who killed the baby's grandfather. Awesome.

I sigh and close my eyes, trying to center my thoughts on something else. It doesn't work. All I can think of is Hayden and his reaction to finding out I'm pregnant. If he was overprotective before, I shudder to imagine how he'd be now.

There's a slim possibility that he'd be less overbearing now that Russell's out of the picture. At least, I assume he is. Given the way Hayden shot both his kneecaps, I don't think I'm wrong.

I'm in love with an insane man.

As if conjured by my thoughts, Hayden steps into the room. My heart drops into my stomach. The last time I saw him, he had a gun in his hand and an unholy rage in his eyes that burned brighter than hellfire. Now he stands just in front of the closed door, wearing a cautious expression.

A thousand thoughts and emotions swirl within me at the sight of him. I clutch the scratchy hospital sheets, willing my hands not to shake.

"How are you feeling?" he asks softly.

Despite everything, I soften a little at the tenderness in his voice. "Honestly? I'm overwhelmed. My head hurts every time I try to make sense of everything until all I want to do is sleep."

Hayden nods, stepping further into the room until he's standing at the foot of the bed. Close but with enough space that my anxiety doesn't spike. "That's understandable, considering what you've gone through."

"Do you know what happened to Sebastian? And there

was a little girl named Erika. She was also there, but she should've gotten away."

"Sebastian has been better. Despite being shot and losing a lot of blood, he'll make a full recovery. The child has been reunited with her mother. Once the girl lured you into the alley, they didn't care about her anymore, and she was fine. Shaken up, but fine. Please don't worry about them. It's you that needs attention, Callie."

"You weren't here when I woke up..." I let the sentence trail off, unable to voice the question I want to ask.

"You know where I was."

I bite the inside of my cheek. "Is he...?"

He nods, the skin along his jaw tightening. "Yes. If they ever find him, they're not going to be able to identify him."

"Good."

Hayden's mouth lifts into a small smile. "That's my girl."

I let out a shaky breath as relief washes over me. Cleansing me. Russell is dead, gone and buried. Although I already suspected that was the case, hearing Hayden confirm it with absolute certainty comforts me in a way I didn't realize I needed.

"He'll never hurt you, or anyone else, ever again," he says.

"I shouldn't be happy, but I am."

Hayden scoffs. "Fuck that guy. No one touches you and lives."

I nod, a lump forming in my throat. As complicated as this situation with Hayden is, I still care for him. Too much.

"Thank you."

"I'd do anything for you," he says. After walking to the side of the bed, he sits down with a long exhale, gazing at me with an unreadable look. "Are you sure you're okay?"

"Yes."

Hayden runs his hand through his hair. "I couldn't let him get away. You know that's why I had to leave, don't you?" When I nod, he continues. "It wasn't only because of that. I couldn't watch you..."

"Die," I say, finishing his sentence.

"Fuck, I can't even say the word, not when it comes to you." He reaches out to touch me, then retracts his arm.

I don't know whether to be relieved or disappointed. "What's wrong?"

Hayden closes his eyes. "I'm afraid that this is all a dream and you're not really alive. That I'm still in that house where my mother died, but instead, I'll find your body there. I can't handle that if it's reality. I can't live without you."

"Hey," I whisper, taking his hand between mine. I shove away the horror churning inside me. It must've been traumatic for Hayden to be there after all these years. I refocus my thoughts because right now he needs reassurance, the same way I needed to know about Russell's death. "I'm fine, Hayden. This is real. We're together, sitting on this bed."

He looks at me, his gaze full of yearning. "Are we really together, Callie?"

I pause. I don't want to lie to him, but I can't give him the answer he wants. "I—I don't know. There's so much we need to discuss, but I don't know if I have the strength to hear it."

"We can do this now or wait until we're home. Giving you the choice is the least I can do."

"Let's have this conversation here," I say with a resolute nod. "That way, if I have a heart attack, I'm in the best possible place to survive it."

He frowns at me while gripping my hand like a lifeline. "That's not funny."

"It wasn't a joke."

"I can't deny that I've done some terrible things and made a few choices that I wish I could take back," he says slowly. "Some of which can't be justified or easily forgiven. But despite everything, I love you, Callie. You're the only thing in my life that makes it worth living. I used to live for justice, but now I live for you."

It takes me several deep breaths to find my ability to form words. Even when I do, they tremble, exposing my inner turmoil. "I don't want anything from you except complete honesty right now. Not some half-truths or lies by omission. I want all of the facts that led you to do what you did."

"I'll explain, but you know all of it already. What Russell said?" Hayden averts his gaze, a streak of pain briefly traveling over his face. "He told you everything. How he set me up to think your father murdered an innocent woman, the exact type of person that I'd be tempted to kill to protect society. It worked. He fooled me, and I took the senator's life. I'll carry that regret with me until I die.

"After my mother's death, I swore to myself that I'd not only avenge her, but any other woman who'd met a similar end. I worked both sides of the law by being an attorney and a criminal, with the one goal of making sure no one guilty got away with such a horrendous crime. My choices, both good and bad, led me to you."

He looks at me and releases my hand to trail his fingers down my cheek. "All of my pain and suffering was worth the chance of meeting you. Never mind the honor of loving you."

"Hayden..." His name is full of the agony inside me. It spills onto every letter.

"I'm truly sorry for what I did," he says, his voice

strained. "I know I don't deserve your forgiveness, but I need it. Just like I need you. Please, Callie."

His blatant desperation is what breaks me.

Tears fill my eyes and spill onto my cheeks. I don't bother wiping them. Not when many more will follow. "I believe you're sorry, and I understand how the pain of losing your mother drove you to do what you did. But understanding doesn't change anything or make it hurt less."

He reaches out to gently brush the tears from my cheeks, raw anguish in his gaze. "You're right." He takes a shaky breath. "What do I do now?"

I wince at the self-loathing written on his face. "I need time. Can you give me that?"

His eyes narrow with displeasure, and my pulse ratchets. "How much do you need?"

"Grief doesn't have an expiration date," I snap. "And neither does forgiveness. You said you'd do whatever it took to win me back, but the second I mention needing some time to myself, you revert to your old self. If you really want to prove that I can trust you, you'll let me go."

He lets out a laugh that holds no amusement. "I don't fucking think so."

CHAPTER 31

C alista

I MAKE MY ESCAPE THE FOLLOWING MORNING WHILE HAYDEN'S at court.

After talking to police about the "incident" and blaming the drugs for my lack of helpful details—*without* pointing them in Hayden's direction—I walk away from the hospital. If only I wasn't wearing the same clothes from before. Seeing them reminds me of Russell and has my stomach churning.

Or maybe it's the pregnancy.

"Please don't cause me problems like your father does, okay?" I whisper to my belly. "I can barely handle one Bennett. I don't need another one making my life difficult."

My breathing goes shallow at the idea of Hayden's reaction when he discovers I'm gone. I might've left him a note so he knows I'm fine, but he's not going to be. Fucking pissed is more accurate.

His possessiveness runs too deep to let me have any real independence. And it's not only my life I'm taking into consideration. Being pregnant has changed everything. I may not be strong enough to walk away from Hayden, but I can and have for this baby.

Until Hayden's ready to change, it's not going to work between us.

That doesn't mean it's not killing me.

My steps are heavy as I walk down the sidewalk and climb into a waiting cab.

"Where to?" the driver asks.

"The bank on the corner of Weston Drive."

"You got it."

I stare blankly out the window, despite the amount of adrenaline coursing through me. My decision to leave Hayden wasn't an easy one to make, but it's the right one. I just wish I could savor this small taste of freedom.

The cab drops me off at the bank first. I head inside and withdraw every single dollar in my account. Going off the grid is hard if you rely on debit cards, and I haven't forgotten Hayden has a hacker on his payroll.

The next place the cab drops me off is the college campus, where I resist the urge to run all the way to the dormitory. Specifically, Harper's. To say she's shocked when she opens the door is an understatement. To say I'm happy to see her is another one.

I throw my arms around her with a small cry. She's quick to return the hug.

"What the fuck did that asshole do?" she asks. "I swear to God if he's hurt you, I'm going to kill him."

The thought of my best friend going up against my boyfriend—ex-boyfriend?—who has actually killed people has a hysterical laugh bubbling up in my chest. She pulls back to stare at me with a frown.

"Uh oh. Let's get you inside. I'm pretty sure it's 5 o'clock somewhere," she mumbles.

I follow her through the doorway, wiping the dampness from my face. The dorm room is small but cozy, with bright string lights hanging from the ceiling and colorful throw pillows on her bed. One wall has been painted a deep purple and is covered in framed prints of impressionist paintings. Her bed has a comforter with a bohemian pattern that matches the fluffy rug. Among the artsy decor, one poster stands out.

"Sarcasm, because punching people is frowned upon," I read out loud with a smile.

Harper shrugs. "It's true though." She sits down and pats the empty spot next to her. "Sit. I know you didn't come here to stare at my awesome poster."

"I wish," I mutter. After I plop onto the mattress, I release a long sigh. "I want to tell you everything, but not right now. Could we pretend to be normal college students for a little while?"

"I didn't think I'd have to get the bong out this soon, but..." At my eyes widening, she laughs. "I'm just kidding. Let's order takeout and watch movies until we're cross-eyed. Does that sound good?"

"It's perfect."

"I've missed you."

I lay my head on her shoulder. "I've missed you more."

Harper orders an epic amount of food—pizza, wings, eggrolls, the works. We settle on her bed surrounded by half-empty cartons and proceed to watch hours and hours' worth of comedies on her laptop. For a little while, we're just a pair of best friends, laughing over silly movies and bad jokes. No dark shadows from my past, no worries beyond overeating and getting sick.

My friend keeps the mood light, sensing how much I need this. Eventually, she pauses the fifth—or sixth?—movie and turns to me.

"So, are you ready to talk about it?" she asks, her tone gentle but cautious.

I nod. "I think so."

She takes my hand, letting me know without words that she's here for me. The words start off slowly, but then spill from me in a rush that's accompanied with tears. Lots of them. I tell her everything, even though it scares me to be this vulnerable with someone about my secrets and Hayden's.

Unlike him, I can trust Harper.

By the time I'm done talking about his remorse and apology, along with my doubts and fears, I'm spent. I flop back onto the mound of pillows and close my eyes, now swollen.

"I just need time and distance to process everything that's happened," I say, "and I don't think he's willing to give that to me, regardless of what he said."

"First of all, pregnant...A Calista barista is on the way. That means I'm going to be an auntie, which is fucking cool. Second, what's your plan? Are you going to continue going to school? Classes start the day after tomorrow."

"Honestly, I feel like I'm in the witness protection program. I left my cell phone at the hospital, and I'm carrying cash so my cards can't be traced. I want to go to school, but I'm scared to go out in public." I slap my forehead. "What the hell can I do?"

Harper lies down beside me and taps my nose. "You're going to stay here until you figure it out. I'll make sure you have access to my laptop, and you can do your courses online. That way, you don't have to go to class and chance him finding you." She stops and purses her lips. "You don't think he'll hurt you, right?"

I shake my head emphatically. "No. He might be crazy, but that's one thing I've never had to worry about."

"Good, because my ninja skills are rusty, bro."

A smile tugs at my mouth. "I don't know how I'd survive all of this without you."

"Shit, me either." She grins back at me. "You can thank me by naming the baby after me."

"I think I can make that happen."

CHAPTER 32

H ayden

"State vs. Johnson," the bailiff announces.

I sit with my leg bouncing underneath the table, ready for this case to end. The uncomfortable wooden chair only adds to my agitation. I didn't want to leave Calista for any reason, but going to jail isn't on my to do list. I need to play by the rules for once.

Especially after torturing and dismembering Thomas Russell.

Despite my foul mood, a smile tilts my lips. Hearing him scream was music to my ears, before I cut his tongue out. Even so, it's a song I've put on repeat in my head. He suffered just like I said he would. If Calista hadn't been waiting for me in the hospital, I would've peeled *all* of his skin off, not most of it...

The judge's voice, high-pitched and nasal, brings me out of my musings. I run my gaze over her and then the jury, taking in their bored expressions while silently commiserating.

My thoughts veer back to Calista within a matter of seconds. I replay our last interaction at the hospital, and my gut twists. The uncertainty and hurt in her gaze as she looked at me from the bed still kills me. I have to make her understand that I'm done with taking the law into my hands. I meant it when I said she was my reason for living.

Revenge and justice don't compare to love and devotion.

By the time I stride through the hospital doors several hours later, I'm ready to get on my knees before Calista if she'll promise not to run. I saw the wariness in her eyes, and I haven't been able to dismiss it. Instinctively, I know that's the reason I've been on edge all day and why I sprint down the hallway to her room instead of walking.

My sweaty palm glides along the handle as I turn it and push open the door. My gaze immediately lands on the empty bed, neatly made as if it's been vacant for some time. A spasm hits my chest when I spot a cell phone sitting atop a white envelope.

With shaking hands, I pocket Calista's abandoned cell phone and pick up the envelope with my name written on it. I open it quickly, despite the trepidation gnawing at my insides. The sensation worsens at the string of pearls I find inside. It's accompanied by a handwritten note.

Hayden,

I need time to process everything. My past. You. Everything. When I'm ready to talk, I'll contact you.

~ Calista

I sink onto the bed with my stomach in knots, clutching the small piece of paper...the only piece of Callie that I have left.

For now.

"I'll always chase you," I say to the empty room. "You can trust that."

If she thinks I stalked her before, she has no idea what's coming.

CHAPTER 33

C alista

"Dude, I can tell you're thinking about him again," Harper says, pointing her lollipop at me. "I guess it's not the end of the world since you're going to be his baby momma."

I groan, thinking about my tattoo. "Don't remind me."

"You could do worse than him. He's Hayden Bennett of House Judicial, the First of His Name, King of the Law, Wrecker of Pussies, the Father of Calista Baristas, the Attorney of the Great Courtroom, the Breaker of Hearts."

"I can't believe you!" I take a pillow and throw it at her. She catches it with a laugh. "How long did it take you to come up with that?" I ask.

"One class period of marketing. Look, I was trying to sell the idea of him, okay?"

"You're ridiculous." I sit on the bed next to her with a sigh. "I'm nervous."

"Yeah, I would be too. That Mr. Bennett is cray-cray."

I shake my head. "Not that. The midterms."

"Oh, right." She pats my hand. "I totally forgot they were this morning. I think I studied too hard. Or was it partied too hard? Either way, it's going to be a rough day."

"I understand the university wants us to take them in person to avoid cheating, but I wish that didn't apply to me."

She gives me a look. "Listen, just go in there wearing a hoodie and sunglasses like every other student who thinks they're a badass, and you'll blend right in. Take the test and then you're done until the end of semester finals. Easy peasy, lemon squeezy."

"More like stressed, depressed, lemon zest."

She laughs and bumps my shoulder with hers. "I forgot about that version. But seriously, it's going to be fine."

I shrug. "I hope so."

It's been two months since I ran from Hayden, leaving nothing behind except a note and my necklace. Two months of hiding and attempting and failing to sort through my tangled emotions. Two months of embracing the life growing within me.

I've been hopeful that Hayden would eventually stop looking for me, at least long enough for me to get my head straight, but deep down, I know better. He promised he'd always chase me, which means he *will* find me.

And learn about the baby.

"Come on," Harper says, getting to her feet. She pulls me into a standing position before opening her dresser drawers. "Try this one. No, this."

I take the Columbia University hoodie and smile at the permanent marker on the sleeves. "I'm not lazy, I'm just motivationally challenged," I read aloud. "I like this one."

She grins at me. "I'm a genius. What can I say?"

A few minutes later, we're both dressed and ready for

class. I take a deep breath and follow Harper from the dorm room, keeping my expression blank despite the nervousness flowing through me. She links her arm through mine as we walk across the quad toward my first class.

"You've got this."

"There are so many people."

She wrinkles her nose. "I know, right? People. Eww."

"That's not what I meant."

"Well, that's what *I* meant."

I help but grin at the disgust in her voice. My amusement quickly fades, and my footsteps slow as we approach the lecture hall doors. Harper stops and turns to face me.

"Hey, look at me," she says gently. When I meet her gaze, she gives me an encouraging smile. "I'll walk with you to every class, and we have the last one together, so you won't be alone all day."

I take a shaky breath. "I'm being stupid. It's not like I saw him or anything."

"That's right. You've got this. Now go and kick some ass. I'll see you afterwards."

With a final wave, she walks down the hall. I turn toward the door, grip my backpack strap, and push the door open. I step over the threshold, scanning every aisle and every corner. When I don't see Hayden anywhere, relief flows through me.

I make my way to the back of the room and settle in, arranging my pens and pencils on the small desktop. The professor walks in a few seconds later. The students fall silent as he folds his arms.

"Let's get this over with," mutters the guy next to me.

I smile to myself.

I couldn't agree more.

Harper looks like she's about to puke.

"This is the last exam for today. Are you ready?" I ask her.

She shrugs. "As ready as I'm going to be. You?"

"Honestly, I'm feeling pretty good about all of my tests so far."

"Good. Then I'll cheat off of you."

I roll my eyes with a smile. "Whatever."

The professor walks in and opens his laptop that's connected to the projector, and on the whiteboard is a timer. "You'll have sixty minutes to complete the test," he says. "I'll start the timer as soon as all of the exams have been distributed."

The T.A. places one in front of me, and I pick up my pencil with trembling fingers. Only this time, I'm less nervous and more excited. This is just another step toward me taking control of my future.

"All right, students, you may begin," he says, clicking a button on the laptop. The timer starts counting down from 60:00.

I write my name at the top and focus on the test, blocking out the people around me. The scratches of pencils and the rustling of papers quickly fade into the background. I work through the questions methodically, keeping an eye on the timer.

With thirty minutes left, I pause to stretch my arms and roll my neck. I delve back in, pushing away thoughts of Hayden whenever they try to creep through my mind.

I'm close to finishing when there's five minutes left. After filling in the final question, I relax and lean back in my chair. The numbers on the projector continue downward until they disappear. Before the time is up a message appears in their place: *"I'll always chase you, Mrs. Bennett."*

I swear my heart stops. The letters seem to pulse and grow, filling my vision completely. There's a series of gasps and whispered words as students begin to notice the change. Dimly, I hear the professor saying that the timer must've malfunctioned, but it's drowned out by the blood roaring in my ears.

Hayden has found me.

I stumble from my seat in a daze when the professor calls time. Clutching my exam to my chest, I hurry over to his desk to turn it in before racing from the classroom. Harper catches up to me in the dorm room.

"What the fuck was that?" she says, her eyes wide. "Never mind. We've got to get you out of here."

When I shake my head, she frowns at me. "At first, I wanted to run away, but there's no point. I have nowhere to go, and I'm tired of hiding. It's been two months, and this is the first time he's contacted me. I think I'm ready to talk to him."

Harper opens her mouth to argue, but I hold up a hand. "Please. I'm not asking you to agree, just to support me. I need to do this. He has a right to know about the baby."

She folds her arms and gives me a pointed look. "You still love him."

I release a hollow laugh. "Yup."

"Okay, but make sure you call me after. That way, I'll know you're okay. If I don't hear from you, I'm calling a hit man. If I don't take him out myself. I know you said he won't hurt you, but he's not above kidnapping."

She's not wrong.

"Agreed," I say. "Can I borrow your phone?"

Harper blows out a breath, disturbing the loose tendrils

around her forehead. "Sure. I'm not going to lie, I'm sad our girl-time is over."

When she hands me her cell phone, I take it with a frown. "You're acting like I'm not coming back."

"Girl, I know you aren't. You're going to take one look at his baby blues, or his dick, and become a puddle on the ground." She holds up her hands. "Not that I blame you. Just make sure it's what *you* want."

"Okay," I whisper. "I promise."

CHAPTER 34

H ayden

My phone chimes with a text from an unknown number. I'm tempted to delete it until I glimpse Calista's name on it.

Finally, after two fucking months, she's ready to talk.

Not without a little push from me. It's no coincidence that she's contacting me right after I ordered Zack to hack into her professor's laptop. But when it comes to her, I'll win no matter what it takes.

After texting her back and agreeing to meet at my penthouse, I set down my phone and put the vehicle in drive. The entire ride to my destination is filled with thoughts of Calista. Like it's been since she disappeared on me.

The worst time of my life.

I vacillated between extreme fear on her behalf and an all-consuming anger that she betrayed me after promising not to run. To be fair, she gave me her word *before* she learned about the part I played in her father's murder, but still.

If she can understand that I did it to protect others, she might forgive me. If she doesn't, I don't know how I'm going to survive it. I'll probably kidnap her again and keep her under lock and key until she changes her mind...

After I've parked my vehicle, I make my way to the elevators in the lobby. As soon as the metal doors shut, visions of me tasting Calista's pussy rise in my mind. I groan.

The memory of her is enough to ruin me.

I push the button for the ground floor, several times, my charged energy spilling from my fingertips. I can't wait to see her again. The pain of waiting is so real that I can't even summon the patience to wait for her in my penthouse.

Every night since I discovered her whereabouts, I've tried to picture how this reunion is going to play out, but with little success. Will she cry and apologize for leaving? Plead with me?

I shake my head at my idiotic thoughts. If anyone is going to beg, it'll be me. I've made my peace with that. When I said I was willing to do anything to have her, it included swallowing my pride.

The time drags until Calista appears. The second my gaze lands on her it's as though all the air is sucked from my lungs, making it difficult for me to breathe. I can't take my eyes off her. Not only because she's beautiful, but I'm worried she'll disappear again.

I follow her every movement from where I stand by the elevators. Although my expression is calm, my heart pounds wildly in my chest as if it wants to place itself in her palm. Would she accept it?

Or crush it?

After her gaze lands on me, I make my way over to her,

my focus never wavering. When our eyes meet, I catch a glimpse of the emotions swirling in hers. Along with sadness and regret is a hardened resolve. She's steeled herself for this encounter.

While I'm dying to touch her.

To kiss her.

It takes all of my willpower not to pull Calista into my arms when I stop in front of her. That doesn't mean I don't inhale deeply to pull the scent of her into my lungs.

"Calista," I greet.

She gives me a curt nod. "Hayden."

I scrutinize her face, desperately searching for a hint of warmth that used to be there when she looked at me. Some faint ember in her hazel eyes that tells me she doesn't hate me completely.

"Why did you leave?" I ask.

That is the question that's invaded my mind every day without fail. Now that I'm about to receive that answer, I'm not certain I'm ready for the truth. What will I do if Calista doesn't care about me anymore?

I'll lose my fucking mind.

"I don't want to do this in public," she says quietly.

After jerking her chin in the direction of the elevators, Calista starts walking. I pivot on my heel to trail after her. If this isn't indicative of our power dynamic, I don't know what is.

I'll follow this woman to the depths of hell or to the heights of heaven. Wherever she goes, I go. Calista can run, but I'll always chase her.

We step inside the elevator and I fist my hand to refrain from grabbing her. The urge is so strong it races through every tendon, every muscle until I'm shaking.

She folds her hands, her expression guarded. "I left

217

because of everything that happened. I had to get away to think, and I knew you wouldn't let me do that in peace."

"So, you ran and scared the shit out of me?" I narrow my eyes at her, silently accusing her for torturing me these past months. "Do you know how worried I've been, the number of sleepless nights I've experienced? I couldn't rest without knowing whether or not you were alive."

"With all that happened, you have to understand that I was falling apart," she says. After folding her arms, she gives me a hard look. "I'll never condone what you did to my father, but the truth is, he killed people. Maybe not directly, but his actions certainly led to a number of deaths. It's taken me months to finally wrap my head around that."

"I never would've taken his life if I had known the truth."

She nods slowly. "I know that now, but only because I've had time to myself."

"And now? Where does that leave us?" I hear the desperation in my voice the second the words leave my mouth.

She averts her gaze. "How did you find me?"

My mouth thins at her attempt to change the subject. "I couldn't at first. Worst fucking weeks of my life. Finally, Zack noticed that all of your professors recorded grades for you after the first six-weeks quiz. Then it wasn't hard to figure out where you were and what you were doing."

"Oh." She scrunches her face. "I'm surprised you didn't contact me sooner."

"You said you wanted time, and I gave you that. But I got tired of waiting. I miss you, Calista. So fucking much."

"Oh." She repeats the word, but this time it's breathy. There's a softening in her gaze, the icy detachment thawing. Her reaction gives me a flicker of hope.

"I'm sorry about everything," I say. "I don't know what

else you want me to say. The only thing I can do is prove it to you."

Her gaze travels over my face, gauging the sincerity of my words. I meet her eyes unflinchingly. I mean everything I've said.

After a moment, she drops her head, breaking eye contact with me. "I'm pregnant."

This tiny whisper hits me with the force of a hurricane. I can only stare at her. My mind is reeling, trying to process the news as I stand there in silence.

If this is true...I might literally die from happiness.

"Say something, Hayden," she snaps. "I'm kind of freaking out over here."

"Let's go."

CHAPTER 35

Calista

"Go?" I repeat. "Go where?"

Hayden doesn't answer me. He simply takes my hand in a tight grip and mashes the shit out of the elevator button that'll take us to the ground floor. I tug on our joined hands to get his attention.

"What are you doing?"

He swings his gaze to me, the blue sparkling with urgency. "I'm taking you to an OB-GYN."

"Why?"

"I have to make sure this is real."

I frown up at him. "And if it is?"

He pauses, almost as though frightened to speak. "If this is actually happening, it's the best day of my life."

Tears prick my eyes. "Really? I know this complicates everything."

"That's why you ran." When I slowly nod, he yanks me

into his arms, wrapping me in a secure embrace. He blows out a harsh breath that sweeps over my temple. "God, Callie, if you weren't pregnant, I'd kidnap you and never let you leave."

"If I weren't pregnant, we wouldn't be having this conversation right now," I say, my words muffled against his coat.

He places a kiss on my hair. "I'm sorry, baby. You must've been scared, but you don't have to worry anymore. I'm here, and I'm not going anywhere."

I pull back and give him a wry smile. "That's what I'm afraid of."

Hayden doesn't speak to me again. But he does communicate with everyone else: telling the driver where to go, ordering the receptionist to fit us in for an emergency appointment, and even demanding that the doctor do a sonogram when we walk into the exam room.

I look at Dr. Sheridan with a shrug. The faster she falls in line, the better off we'll all be.

"It's good to see you again," she says to me. "Why don't you lie down, Miss Gr—"

"*Mrs. Bennett*," Hayden says.

"My apologies." She looks at me with a calm expression. That makes one of us. "Mrs. Bennett, please lie down and lift your shirt to expose your stomach."

I do as she says, my nerves bouncing inside me. Hayden stands beside me like a sentry on duty, his jaw set in a hard line.

The doctor squirts a cool gel on my belly and guides the ultrasound wand across my skin. The room is silent except for the whooshing sound of the baby's heartbeat. The tears that have been threatening to fall since I first saw Hayden again trail down my cheeks.

I don't have the gumption to tell him this is the first time

I'm going to see the baby because I was hiding. Although I've done everything else to protect him or her. It helps that Harper practically shoved prenatal vitamins down my throat.

"There we go," Dr. Sheridan says gently.

An image appears on the screen, irrevocably changing my life. Our baby, nestled safely inside me. Tiny arms that will one day wrap around us. And tiny legs that will one day run to us.

Hayden takes my hand in his trembling one. He turns to me, his rough exterior finally cracking. "That's our baby," he whispers brokenly.

My heart swells. In this moment, the darkness of our past doesn't matter. All I see is the family we're becoming. I was lonely for so long, but not anymore.

Never again.

"Yes," I whisper. "That's our baby."

The doctor clears her throat. "I'll give you two some time alone."

She leaves the room, but neither of us acknowledge her, both of us too caught up in each other and the life we've created.

"This is really happening," Hayden says, his voice full of wonder.

"I'm sorry I hid this from you."

He nods slowly and lifts my hand to press a kiss to my knuckles. "I forgave you the moment you told me."

His immediate acceptance takes me by surprise. I wipe my damp cheeks and attempt to smile at him. It wobbles on my face. "I was scared," I say softly. "Scared of how you'd react. Of what you might do..."

"You were right to worry."

My eyes widen. "What do you mean?"

"I don't want to do this in public."

I FIGHT NAUSEA THE ENTIRE DRIVE BACK TO HAYDEN'S PENTHOUSE. AND it's not because I'm pregnant. My nerves zip along my arms and legs until I feel like I've stuck a fork in an electric socket.

The minute we step inside the living room, I whirl to face him, unable to stand the heavy silence between us. "Why did you say that I should've been worried?"

His gaze pierces mine, unwavering and unapologetic. "Because you know who I really am and what I'm capable of."

I swallow the lump in my throat. "What does that mean exactly?"

"You and this baby are all I've ever wanted, all I ever dreamed of having. For you to take that from me..." He shakes his head and briefly closes his eyes. "You must hate me to hurt me that much."

"I never meant to. I know I did inadvertently, but it wasn't my intention." I reach out to grasp his hand. "Please believe me."

Hayden pulls me to him and I go willingly, unable to resist the pull he has on me. After cupping my cheek, he places his thumb along my jaw to hold me in place. "I do believe you."

I scrunch my face in confusion. "Then why did you say that you didn't want to do this in public? What is 'this'?"

"Fuck you."

My lips part on a gasp. Hayden is quick to take advantage of my surprise, slamming his mouth to mine, his tongue driving between my lips. My pulse accelerates even more when he wraps his arm around my back and forces our bodies together. His cock digs into my belly, making my pussy flutter.

I pull away first to suck air into my lungs. His eyes burn with hunger and passion, a bright flame that steals the breath I just took. When I start to say something, his fingers dig into my hip to stop me.

Hayden hauls me into the hallway and slams my back against the wall. He covers my body with his, pressing into me, the heat of his skin burning me. Sweat breaks out on my forehead and my cheeks grow flushed, but it's nothing compared to the fevered look in his eyes.

I can taste the fire in his kiss and feel it in his demanding grip. My head is swimming when he finally jerks his head back. He grinds into me and I moan softly. His nostrils flare as he devours me with his gaze, his hands roaming my body. I've been starved for his touch.

For him.

He slides his hand into my hair and fists a handful. His touch makes me shiver and I turn my head to give him better access. "I'm going to fuck you so hard that you won't be able to walk, let alone run from me," he murmurs, the sound rumbling in his chest. "First I'm going to own this pussy. Then I'm going to own you."

He lifts his gaze to mine, his dark, brooding eyes bright with his near-insanity. He grabs my jaw, forcing me to meet his stare. "Do you hear me, Mrs. Bennett?"

"Yes, Mr. Bennett."

His hold on me grows tight enough to bruise. He doesn't give me time to recover, slamming his mouth back onto mine. I kiss him back, sliding my arms around his neck, and arch into him, rubbing my breasts against his hard chest.

Hayden pulls away with a hiss. He swings me into his

arms and marches toward the bedroom. His strength and determination make me weak. I lie helpless but eager in his embrace until he sets my feet on the floor.

Then he's ripping my clothes from my body. I wince at first, but soon every sound of material being torn fills me with anticipation. Hayden's violent actions have me trembling by the time I'm naked.

He freezes. He stares. And then he sinks to his knees before me.

"Hayden, what...?"

He grips the backs of my thighs, his fingers digging into my skin, and leans forward to place a lingering kiss on my tattoo. Followed by my slightly rounded belly. "If you told me to crawl, I would. If you told me to die for you, I would. And if you tell me to live for you, I will." He presses his cheek against my thigh with an exhale. "I'll do anything for you and this baby, Callie."

I run my fingers through his hair while my emotions threaten to choke me. "I don't want to be responsible for that kind of power over you."

"You already are."

"I'm sorry," I whisper.

Hayden rises, the muscles in his arms and shoulders straining the material of his shirt. "I'm not. Because you're mine. You're always going to be mine. I will always chase you and bring you back to me."

My throat aches, and the tears in my eyes make my vision blurry. "You're willing to chase me forever?"

"Yes. I'm willing to fight for you. Because you're worth it."

"I love you." It's all I can manage, but it's everything I have.

He makes a pained sound as his hands slide up my

rib cage. He palms my breasts and my nipples harden against his palms. I tilt my head back to accommodate the deep, bruising kiss he gives me. It's punishing. It's desperate.

It's beautiful.

Hayden guides me down onto the bed and I stare up at him, unable to look away. He skims his thumb over my tattoo. His branding of me.

"Do you know why I did this?" When I don't answer, he continues. "Because I loved seeing my last name on your skin. Because I wanted to see it every time I fucked you."

I smile at his arrogance and lift my arms to him. He unbuttons his shirt with his usual efficiency and then his pants. Once he's on top of me, he uses one arm to cage me in and the other to stroke my inner thigh. His touch leaves a trail of fire in its wake.

Hayden's mouth lands on mine with a fury. He kisses me as if he's punishing me and I kiss him back because I like the way he dominates me.

"You're so fucking perfect," he says against my lips.

And then his fingers are sliding through my slit, making me moan into his mouth. I suck his lower lip between my teeth and bite. Hard.

Hayden pulls away with a grin, his dark eyes gleaming. "So you do want to play dirty, huh?" He slides his hand under my knee and lifts my leg into the air.

"What are you—?"

He grinds his cock against my clit. "I love how your body comes alive for me, baby."

My body is vibrating. My heart is beating out of control. I want to scream and beg for more.

Hayden places a kiss on my jaw before trailing his lips along my neck, biting occasionally. "I love how responsive you are." His hand slides to my thigh and squeezes it hard. "I love how easily I can make you come."

He drives into me, hard enough to hurt. I whimper in his embrace. Hayden groans against my ear. "You feel so fucking good."

I gasp when he withdraws and then slams into me again. He starts moving faster and harder, his fingers digging into my skin to hold me still. But it's not enough. I need more.

I need everything he has to give me.

"Please," I whisper.

He doesn't say a word, his tongue delving in my mouth as he fucks me. He goes faster and harder with every thrust. I can feel the tingling of my skin, the warm ache deep in my belly. The pressure inside me grows until I can barely breathe.

I hold on to him, my nails digging into his skin as I chase after my release. The pleasure is intense and overwhelming, and I want to cry out from the sheer ecstasy of it.

Hayden breaks away from my mouth. "Look at me."

I open my eyes to find his. They're hooded and dark with lust, but still focused on mine. "Come for me, Mrs. Bennett," he demands.

I can't refuse him. His gaze holds me captive until I tip over the edge. I moan and arch against him, my body writhing on his as I'm swept away in a tidal wave of euphoria. My orgasm rolls over me in crashing waves that leave me panting.

Hayden continues to drive into me until he's gripping me hard and his cock jerks inside me. Then he's coming, his mouth devouring mine as he shudders from the pleasure.

It takes a few moments for him to still, and when he does, he stares at me, his eyes searching mine. He rolls onto his back and takes me with him. I curl into his chest, feeling his heart thump under my cheek.

"I've missed everything about you," he says softly, running his fingers through my hair. "The taste of you, the noises you make when I'm inside you. The way you bite your lip and moan my name. Every fucking thing."

He brushes a strand of hair from my face, his expression unreadable.

I frown. "What's wrong?"

"I didn't want this with you, you know," he says. "The amount of control you had over me from the beginning..." He laughs softly. "It's worse now with the baby, but I've never been happier."

He pauses, his brows gathering. "Actually, I don't think I've ever been truly happy. Until you." He pulls me closer and kisses me, soft and gentle. "Thank you for giving me that."

I close my eyes and press my cheek to his chest. His words make my heart so full that it hurts. But I wouldn't change a thing.

"Do you know what else you could do to make me happy?" he asks.

I lift my head and stare down at him with a playful smile. "Haven't I done enough? I mean, I'm going to have your baby for fuck's sake."

"Language, Mrs. Bennett."

I pinch his chest and he laughs. "Fine," I say with a huff. "What do you want?"

"Marry me."

My mouth falls open. "What?"

"Marry me," he repeats, more firmly.

"Is this because of the baby?"

He gives me an exasperated look. "No, because I love

you. Because you're mine." He runs his fingers over my tattoo in a caress. "Because I want you in every way I can get you."

I bite my lip, my nerves firing off inside me. He lifts his head to nibble on my lips until I moan. "Say, yes, Callie. If not, I'm going to fuck you until you do."

My sigh is loud, but the beating of my heart is louder. "Yes."

His mouth captures mine. He kisses me like he owns me. And he does.

His fingers wrap around the back of my neck as he stares into my eyes. "Let's go."

"Wait, what?"

He kisses me again before pulling back with a smile, one so bright and beautiful that my heart melts. "When the woman of your dreams says she wants to marry you, you don't let anything get in the way of her changing her mind."

Keep reading for an exclusive look into

HAYDEN & CALISTA'S
HAPPY EVER AFTER

CHAPTER 1

C alista

Calista: Friend…

Harper: WTF DID HE DO?! He's a dead man for sure this time.

Calista: It's nothing bad. He wants to get married.

Harper: Of course he does. That man tattooed his last name on your body. I know you're blind with love and all that shit, but come on…

Calista: You're right. So, do you want to be my maid of honor?

Harper: FUCK YES! Do you even need to ask? Seriously.

Calista: <3. Can you meet up at the court house on Smith Ave in two hours?

Harper: So, what was it?

Calista: What was what?

Harper: What convinced you to say yes? His baby blues or his dick?

Calista: Both.

Harper: LOL Finally, caliente Calista is back. I'll be there. Do I need to get a dress?

Calista: No, I'm wearing your hoodie.

Harper: Haha that's awesome. Please tell me you're going to do a real wedding at some point? You deserve it.

Calista: We will.

Harper: Okay, then you have my blessing to proceed. See you in a little bit. If you don't want to do this, just flip me off. That can be our distress signal.

Calista: There are times when I think I don't deserve you.

Harper: You do. And more.

CHAPTER 2

C alista

An Hour Later...

> Calista: *sends pic

Harper: Holy fuckballs. Is that a diamond?

> Calista: Lol. Yes. Hayden wanted me to have a wedding ring.

Harper: As he should. However, that's not a ring, that's a fucking satellite. Bro, the second it catches the sunlight and reflects it into space aliens are going to come and abduct your ass.

> Calista: You and Hayden won't let that happen.

Harper: Fair.

> Calista: See you soon!

> Harper: Yeah, assuming your hand doesn't fall off. Xoxo

HAYDEN STARES AT ME LIKE I'M NAKED. I SQUIRM UNDER HIS perusal with a shy smile tugging at my lips.

"Nervous?" he asks.

I shake my head. "Should I be?"

"No." He takes my left hand and lifts it toward his face. "This is really happening."

His whisper grazes my skin, leaving it tingling. "Sometimes, I can't believe you're mine."

"Almost."

He raises a brow. "What did I tell you about the word 'almost'?" When I shrug at him, he says, "Apparently, someone wants to *almost* come tonight."

I blink up at him, lips parted on a gasp. "Please don't."

"Then tell me you're mine."

I get on my tiptoes and sweep my lips across his. "I'm yours."

"God, can't the two of you keep it in your pants for more than five minutes?"

Hayden and I swing our gazes to Harper as she marches over to where we stand. "All right. Let's do this," she says.

Hayden shares a look with the judge, who clears her throat and begins the ceremony. Her words flow past me like a breeze, barely penetrating my psyche. How can they when Hayden stares at me the entire time, his gaze holding promises?

Some full of love.

Some sensual.

But all of them real.

"Is there any reason these two should not be joined in matrimony?" the judge asks.

Harper opens her mouth, and Hayden's eyes narrow to little more than slits. I shoot my best friend a pleading look because I don't want Hayden to lose his shit. She grins at me.

"Proceed," Hayden snaps.

"By the power invested in me," the judge says, her voice shaking, "I now pronounce you Mr. and Mrs. Bennett."

I'm not even sure if she gives Hayden permission to "kiss the bride" before he snatches me to him. It's so quick that I don't have time to do more than breathe. And then I'm kissing him back, pouring my love and devotion into the act.

"Good thing you're already pregnant," Harper mutters, "or else you might be in trouble tonight."

Hayden pulls back, just enough to whisper, "Who says we're waiting until then?"

"Listen, Mr. Bennett," Harper says, "there's something you should know."

"Which is?"

My best friend looks at me. "Tell him about the baby's name."

"Okay, so I made this promise..."

CHAPTER 3

C alista

Two Years Later...

"HARPER."

The redhead winks at me. "You rang, bridezilla?"

I shake my head with a laugh. "Not you." I swing my gaze to the toddler with a crown of flowers resting on her black hair. "Come here, baby."

My daughter skips over to me, her blue eyes bright with excitement. "Ready?"

I take her hand in mine and brush back a stray lock of hair. "Yes, it's time. Remember to listen to your auntie Harper, okay?" She nods so enthusiastically that my heart swells in my chest. "That's my girl."

"Come on, Harper the Second," my best friend says, steering my daughter toward the door. "We've got some sh— erm...things to do."

I shoot her a grateful look. I'm not quite ready for my two-year-old to curse. At least not on my wedding day.

Which ends up being the best day of my life.

Especially when Hayden lifts our Harper into his arms and holds her throughout the ceremony. She immediately snuggles up to his chest with a sigh, the same way I do. That's what my husband does: makes me feel safe.

Because I know the lengths he'll go to protect me.

And our daughter.

God help her first boyfriend...

The pastor looks at me expectantly. "It's time to exchange rings."

"I want one," little Harper says.

After putting my ring on my finger, Hayden kisses her forehead. "I will buy you one, baby. A purity ring," he mutters.

I press my lips together to keep from laughing while I put his ring on his finger. My best friend walks up to take my daughter when it's time for Hayden to kiss me. He pulls me close, but pauses right before his lips find mine.

"Mrs. Bennett?"

I run my fingers over the pearls resting on around my neck. "Yes, Mr. Bennett?"

"Remember that I will always chase you."

"Good."

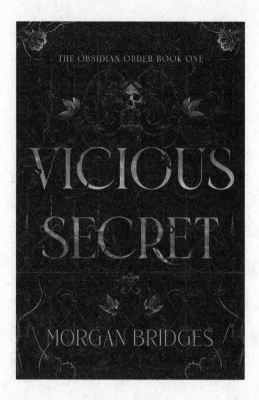

THE OBSIDIAN ORDER BOOK ONE

VICIOUS SECRET

MORGAN BRIDGES

Mors solum initium

Death is only the beginning.

The Recruit

The Obsidian Order only cares about three things: secrecy, loyalty, and power. Every man born to the founding families is bred for this purpose, to serve the society and its objectives.

As a result, we are the elite. Untouchable. Unbreakable. If we make it through the Trials. I will, as long as my obsession doesn't get the best of me. This girl…

If the Order doesn't kill me, she'll be the death of me. Because I won't give her up. She's mine.

The Bride

All I want is my freedom and some coffee. And to find my foster brother. Every clue that leads me closer to Ben only frightens me more.

Something dark and dangerous rules this campus. Similar to the stranger I keep running into. The one I can't stop thinking about. Xavier tells me to stay away from him, but then I'm snared in a game of shadows and savagery.

Now the only way to survive lies in the arms of a man I once tried to kill. The same one who's made me his property. His bride.

Amor est finis

Love is the ending.

The Crow

The Obsidian Order demands not just survival but submission. Every trial, every secret unearthed, binds me deeper to this clandestine world where power is currency and loyalty is conditional.

Yet beneath the surface, a rebellion simmers within me. And Delilah, my obsession, my bride, is the reason. I vowed to protect her, to fight for her.

But can I defy the very Order that shaped me? For my little raptor, I'd take on the world. Because she is everything.

The Raptor

Freedom was once a simple dream. Now it's complicated by the web of intrigue and danger spun around me. Finding Ben was supposed to answer questions, not multiply them. Not only within reality, but within myself.

Xavier, the man whose name is synonymous with both violence and death, has become my protector. Bound by my contract, we navigate this dark labyrinth together, except the Bride Hunt was just the beginning. Now, we must fight not just for our love, but for our very lives.

ACKNOWLEDGMENTS

To my Lord and Savior, Jesus Christ. I'm a hot mess and you love me anyway, so thank you.

To my family. Thank you for being understanding while I was working and unable to be mentally present. Thank you for giving me the opportunity to provide a life that dreams are made of.

To my author friends. Kym (my work wife): I couldn't have gotten this far without your unfailing love and encouragement. This win belongs to you as well. Milana (my work husband): Thank you for being a fortress when I needed protection and for kicking my ass when I needed tough love. I salute you. Elli: Thank you for all of our coaching sessions. They've been life-changing and I wouldn't be this better version of myself without your patience and guidance. This duet is physical manifestation of your belief in me. Luna: Thank you for bringing Hayden to life. This duet wouldn't have been possible without you and your brilliant mind. To the other authors in the community: There are so many of you who I've interacted with and who, in some way, have brought me to this point. Thank you for having an impact on me, regardless of how big or small.

To my BookTokers. To the ladies who took a chance on a "new to them" author by reading my book and then posting videos and pictures of it on social media. Your love for my work gave me the courage to believe in myself again after so many failures. Thank you for sharing your beautiful enthusiasm with me and other readers.

To the Forever team. Sabrina Flemming, editor: Thank you for being a champion behind my books. I never dreamed of this opportunity, and now that it's here, I can't help but see you as the catalyst for my traditional publishing success. Anjuli Johnson, production editor; Estelle Hallick, publicist and marketer; Carolina Martin, advertising manager; Eric Arroyo, production coordinator; Becky Maines, proofreader; Martina Rethman, manufacturing coordinator; Daniela Medina, art director; Leah Hultenschmidt, publisher: Your contribution to this duet means everything to me, and I can't help but express how much I recognize your time and effort. Thank you for all you've done to get this into bookstores and the hands of readers.

To my agent. Jessica Alvarez: Thank you for representing me, answering all of my ridiculous questions, and being so kind about everything.

To my readers. I wouldn't be an author without you. Like Hayden said to Callie, "You mean everything to me."

About the Author

Morgan Bridges is a lover of anti-heroes, deep and thought-provoking books with beautifully written words, romance that's sigh-worthy, scenes that are so hot she blushes, and heroines that inspire her to the point she wants to take their place.

You can find out more at:
authormbridges.com
TikTok @morganbridgesauthor
Instagram @mbridges_author
Facebook @MorganBridgesAuthor